PROJECT
ME 2.0

ALSO BY JAN GANGSEI

THE WILD BUNCH

PROJECT ME 2.0

JAN GANGSEI

ALADDIN

NEW YORK LONDON TORONTO SYDNEY NEW DELHI

ALADDIN

An imprint of Simon & Schuster Children's Publishing Division

1230 Avenue of the Americas, New York, New York 10020

First Aladdin hardcover edition April 2019

Text copyright © 2019 by Jan Gangsei

Jacket illustration copyright © 2019 by Octavi Navarro

Also available in an Aladdin MAX paperback edition.

All rights reserved, including the right of reproduction in whole or in part in any form.

ALADDIN and related logo are registered trademarks of Simon & Schuster, Inc.

For information about special discounts for bulk purchases, please contact Simon & Schuster Special Sales at 1-866-506-1949 or business@simonandschuster.com.

The Simon & Schuster Speakers Bureau can bring authors to your live event.

For more information or to book an event contact the Simon & Schuster Speakers Bureau at 1-866-248-3049 or visit our website at www.simonspeakers.com.

Jacket designed by Jessica Handelman

Interior designed by Mike Rosamilia

The text of this book was set in Adobe Caslon Pro.

Manufactured in the United States of America 0319 FFG

10 9 8 7 6 5 4 3 2 1

Library of Congress Control Number 2018961615

ISBN 978-1-5344-2046-5 (hc)

ISBN 978-1-5344-2045-8 (pbk)

ISBN 978-1-5344-2047-2 (eBook)

For Ted.
Today's the day!

NAME YOUR MOST EMBARRASSING MOMENT.

Go ahead, think about it. Everybody's got one, right? Take my best (okay, make that my *former*) best friend, Burt Miller. He skied straight into a ditch on a field trip to Mount Racer last winter and laughed so hard he peed his pants. Had to ride the bus back to school with his jacket tied around his waist to hide the wet mark. Now he'll be forever known as Burt the Squirt.

Then there's my other buddy, Josh Chan. His dad backed over the statue of our school mascot, Skippy the Squirrel, with his SUV while dropping Josh off at soccer practice last year. Granted, Mr. Chan kinda did us all a favor because: (1) what sort of mascot is a squirrel anyway? and (2) if you're going to have a dorky mascot like a squirrel, at least pick a fiercer name than Skippy. Like Thor.

Still, there's that whole guilt-by-parental-association thing that happens when you're eleven, and let's just say it was a couple of weeks before the sixth grade stopped chattering like dying squirrels every time they saw Josh coming down the hall.

Then there's me—and the reason why I'm here, in my room, where I intend to stay forever. That's right, *forever*. But that's not exactly a short story. So while you're thinking of yours, settle in, and I'll share my own sad and sorry tale. . . .

"The path to enlightenment *does not* include being stuck behind four walls!" a voice interjects. A set of pixelated eyes stare pleadingly at me. "The path to enlightenment begins . . ."

Grrr . . . I glare back at the annoying pest in my old sea monkey tank, his tiny face pressed against the plastic wall of his makeshift prison.

(Yes, you heard that correctly; I have a miniature man—a very horrible, wreck-your-life, not-at-all-genie kind of miniature man—trapped inside a sea monkey tank on my desk.) Don't worry. I'll get to that. But first let's rewind.

Oh, and a bit of advice? When your parents tell you to be careful what you do on the Internet?

Well, I highly suggest you listen.

1

I GUESS YOU COULD SAY THIS WHOLE DISASTER started right where most monumental things in my life do (the great prank call caper of fifth grade, the incredible exploding Mentos experiment, and of course the epic Extreme Smelly Sock™ battle)—in my aforementioned *former* best friend Burt's room.

So there we were, the first Wednesday of summer break, sitting on Burt's top bunk checking out the latest *Dr. Fantastic and the Planet of Doom*. There's nothing better than a brand-spanking-new *Dr. Fantastic*. You know, while it's still fresh and crisp. Before it gets all smudged and bent and crinkled around the edges and starts looking like the stuff you stick in the bottom of a hamster cage.

Only problem was, I couldn't see a thing. Not with my end of the bunk sagging about two hundred feet lower than Burt's, leaving me staring at the bottom of his stinky right foot. To make matters worse, Burt had been pretty much hogging the brand-new comic ever since we'd picked it up at Grady's Grocers that morning.

"Ooh, check out Dr. Fantastic's new super laser blaster of destruction," Burt said. "Lord Dracor is so going down!"

I leaned in closer and held out my hand. "Cool! Let me have it a minute!"

"Uh-uh." Burt shook his head. "Get your own!"

Yeah, okay. In my dreams. With my allowance I could afford maybe one a month. Not one per week like Burt here.

"C'mon, just for a minute, Squirt!"

Burt stuck out his tongue and held the *Dr. Fantastic* to his chest.

"Okay, how about *one second*! C'mon!"

Burt held the shiny comic over his head and smirked. "Nope!"

"Well, now you're asking for it!"

I launched myself full force right at Burt. The bunk bed frame rattled and banged on the wall, and he yelped. Something below us creaked ominously. I ignored that and pinned Burt by the chest with my left arm. My right arm stretched toward the *Dr. Fantastic*.

Burt wiggled to the side, and I brought a giant leg down on him with a *thump*.

Ha! Almost got it . . .

"What the . . . ?" Burt's eyes grew wide. The mattress sank, the creaking grew louder, Burt started to scream, and . . .

Slam!

Burt and I fell straight down with a *thud*. A pile of pillows and blankets landed in a heap on top of us. For a split second we stayed frozen in stunned silence.

Finally, Burt yelled, "Holy cow!" and squirmed his way out from under me. Then we both looked up in shock. All that was left of Burt's bed was the corner of a sheet that got tangled around the top post and hung there like a flag of surrender. Fortunately, Burt's little brother, Darren, had vacated the bottom bunk about a half hour earlier with his Pokémon card collection jammed in his back pocket. Otherwise we'd have been sitting on top of a pest sandwich.

Burt caught his breath and let out a loud whistle. "Holy cow!" he said again. "Maybe you ought to lay off the dough-nuts for once!"

"Maybe you should've just let me have the *Dr. Fantastic* for once!" I snapped back, my face turning hot and my mouth dry and sticky. I had a sudden craving for a nice cold glass of cherry Kool-Aid. And a Tastykake.

I licked my lips and coughed. Only one proven way to defuse a situation like this—I lifted my right leg and let a real honker rip.

Burt cracked up, yanked a blanket over his head, and yelled, "Ack!"

"You're welcome!" I said. Burt snorted and laughed even harder.

Well, you didn't expect anything less from a guy named Farley, now, did you?

That's right, *Farley*. As in Fart, Fartley, Farty. Take your pick.

Just don't ask what Mom and Dad were thinking when they saddled me with that name. Maybe Mom was still delirious after delivering me in the front seat of our car (unmedicated, just ask her!), while she and Dad were stuck in a traffic jam caused by a runaway herd of cows that decided the middle of Route 2A was the best place to stop and chew their cud. (As a result, the framed baby photo over our fireplace features yours truly dressed in a hooded cow onesie and posed next to a barn. Yeah, try living that down.)

Unfortunately, that wasn't all Mom and Dad did.

In a move sure to cement my status as village jester, Mom and Dad were thoughtful enough to give me the middle name Andrew. Now, Andrew's a pretty good name actually. My grandpa's name. And my grandpa's awesome. He can stick his tongue right between his gums and top teeth. And if he gets sick of listening to someone, all he has to do is turn down those speakers in his ears and smile and nod. I wish I could do that. There must be a million situations where that skill would come in handy. For example . . .

Burt stuck his head out from beneath the blanket, yelled, "Is it safe to come out? Ack, nope!" and dodged back under.

So on its own, Andrew would be nothing to complain about. But here's the thing—my last name's Turner.

Think about that one a minute: Farley Andrew Turner. F-A-T.

FAT.

My name spells fat.

And, in case you haven't figured it out yet, I'm not exactly *small*. "Husky" is what my mom likes to say. But I'm not stupid. I know what that means. There's a reason all my pants have elastic in the waist.

I cleared my throat and poked Burt's fleece-covered back. "Think we can fix it, Squirt?" I said hopefully.

Burt pulled the blanket off his head, stopped laughing, and wiped his eyes. We silently surveyed the damage. It looked like someone had just smashed the bunks together with a giant mallet. A colossal game of Whac-A-Mole gone wrong.

"Yeah, I don't think so," Burt said. "I flunked industrial arts class. I'm not allowed around the power tools."

"Right," I said. "Well, we might be able to just wedge the mattress back up there."

Burt shrugged. "Yeah, maybe. Worth a try, I guess. C'mon, give me a hand."

We each grabbed an end of the saggy mattress and heaved it up in the air. Man, this thing was awfully heavy. Maybe it wasn't *entirely* my fault it fell down.

"Almost there," I panted, shoving my end into the upper frame. "Just a little bit more . . ."

Suddenly, Burt dropped his side, and in an instant it *thunk*ed right back onto the bottom bunk. My end slipped off the bed and bonked me on the head.

"Ow! What the heck, Squirt?" I rubbed my noggin.

Burt didn't answer. He peered out the window, between his blue and white soccer ball curtains. I looked too. A big yellow moving truck had pulled up to the curb across the street and was spitting out chairs, beds, tables, and boxes.

"Yeah. Big deal. Trucks stopped being exciting when I turned five. Sheesh." I seized the opportunity to grab the crumpled *Planet of Doom* from the rubble and have a seat on the floor. I flipped to where we'd left off on page twelve. Finally!

"Huh," Burt said, still staring outside. "I didn't think they were coming until next month. . . ."

I closed the comic, leaned forward, and narrowed my eyes. Then I saw who Burt was talking about. She stood at the end of the driveway, bouncing a basketball. Even though she was taller, her hair wasn't in pigtails anymore, and she wasn't wearing a Hello Kitty T-shirt, I'd recognize her anywhere.

"Wait," I said. "Is that . . . *Anna Murphy*?" Without warning, my voice cracked.

Burt nodded. "Yeah. Mom said something about them transferring back here this summer."

Burt's mom is a Realtor and has sold pretty much every house in this town, so she'd know. In fact, if you ever happen to be in Middleford, Massachusetts (home of the Flying Squirrels!), you're quite apt to see Mrs. Miller's giant hair-sprayed head go cruising by on the side of a bus, the back of a moving van, or the bottom of a shopping cart seat. She's the closest thing to a real-life celebrity we've got around here.

"And you didn't tell me?"

Burt, Anna, and I had been pretty much best buds all through preschool, kindergarten, and first grade (the year Anna convinced Burt to let her cut his hair—aka "The Year of the Hat"). We used to build sandbox forts together, catch toads in the woods behind Burt's house, and yeah—watch *Dr. Fantastic* cartoons.

"Guess I forgot." Burt shrugged. "I mean, it's been, like, what, seven years since they left?"

Actually, five. Five years since Colonel Murphy got a new assignment, and Anna and her family left town. Which also made it five years since I'd stuffed a small, unsigned paper heart into Anna's backpack on the last day of school. My cheeks burned at the memory.

Anna's red curls sparkled in the sun as she turned and shot the ball toward the hoop over the garage.

Swish!

My stomach did a funny little flip.

Burt smoothed out his shirt and stood up straight. "We should probably go out and say, 'hey,' right?"

"Huh? No," I said, catching my breath. "No!"

"No? Why not?"

I had to think fast. I wasn't prepared for this. "I mean, they're probably busy. We don't want to get in the way. Besides, we've already wasted too much valuable *Dr. Fantastic* time trying to fix this bed. My mom will be here soon to get me."

I rolled my eyes at Burt and punched his leg. He hesitated a moment, then let out a sigh and flopped down next to me.

"You're right, Fart." He snatched the comic off my lap. "Oh man. What would I do without you?"

"Beats me," I said.

But here's the sad truth: I didn't want to go out there and welcome Anna back to the neighborhood with Burt at my side. See, the thing about Burt is, even though he does goofy stuff like fall in ditches and pee his pants on field trips, he's the kind of guy all the girls like. And I mean *like* like. When Burt falls in a ditch, a half dozen girls in puffy jackets show up to help him out.

If I fell in a ditch, sure, I'd draw a crowd. And I'd probably even get a helping hand or two. But that would be thanks to my highly realistic beached-whale impression that was making everyone laugh.

I inspected Burt sitting there with the comic on his lap, scratching his armpit while chewing his bottom lip, and wondered how he did it. How he'd become *that guy*.

I mean, it's not like Burt looks all that different than he did when we were ten. Okay, so maybe he's taller and probably covered in a little less mud. But he's still got those same skinny legs with the bruised knees, the same messy hair, the same little gap between his two front teeth, and that tiny bump by his right ear.

Burt turned his head in my direction and caught me staring at him.

"Don't even think about it, Fart!" He smirked. His hand shot back up in the air. The comic book flew around again, glossy pages flapping against one another.

But this time I knocked him flat with one push and grabbed the *Dr. Fantastic*.

Yeah, still the same scrawny Burt.

Almost.

It's just that something happened last year about halfway through sixth grade. Something I can't explain. Like a switch got flipped inside Burt, and all the girls in our class turned into a bunch of moths swarming a flame. Next thing you know, Addison Jenkins is passing him notes in homeroom to see if he likes girl A, B, or C, just 'cause she happens to be doing some sort of survey on the subject. And suddenly his phone starts buzzing all the time after school, and there's a Snapchat of Addison's new puppy surrounded by hearts filling the screen and a couple of dancing teddy bears wearing top hats.

My phone doesn't ring.

I don't get notes.

I definitely don't get teddy bears.

I guess nobody bothered to flip on the Farley switch.

Either that or I didn't come with one installed in the first place.

And that was the problem.

Everyone around me was changing—Burt, obviously; Josh, who had grown three inches last summer and scored a spot on the travel soccer team; and even Anna, who was covered in finger paint the last time I saw her and now was . . . well, not a little kid anymore.

But I was still Class Clown Farley, the one famous for running around the gym and popping kickballs just by sitting on them. The one who tried to light his own fart for the general amusement of Cabin 5 at Camp Fun-N-Sun. (Note: I don't recommend this trick at all. One, fire hurts. Two, trying to explain a burn mark in the back seat of your nylon shorts to your mother is not easy.)

And there was no way *that guy* was marching outside to welcome Anna Murphy—the coolest kid in our kindergarten class—back to the neighborhood.

But!

I sat up straight. Now that I thought about it, maybe it didn't have to be that guy reintroducing himself to Anna.

Maybe it could be somebody totally new.

After all, Anna had no idea what had become of

Farley during those five years she was gone. I could have become *anybody*.

And I had the whole summer to do just that. Seven entire weeks before school started to wipe the slate clean and write myself a new story—with yours truly as the *hero*, not the comic relief.

How hard could that be, right?

2

THERE WERE ONLY A COUPLE PLACES WHERE A guy like me could go to transform himself. And thanks to the unfortunate sea monkey mishap when I was nine, I'm no longer allowed to buy anything ever again from the back of a *Dr. Fantastic*. In my defense, how was I supposed to know that putting them into Dad's favorite cooler with five gallons of Gatorade wouldn't make them grow any faster—it just made a very sticky blue mess that I got the "privilege" of cleaning up.

So I decided to stick with the Internet, where I couldn't get into any trouble (ha!).

When I got home from Burt's, I hurried to my room and sat at my desk, eager to get started. I powered up my computer and pecked out "s-e-l-f-i-m-p-r-o-v-e-m-e-n-t." My pointer finger attached itself to something sticky on the *t*. Gross. I licked the tip and tried to wipe away the gooey stuff. Fudge, I was pretty sure. A string of *ttttttttttt*'s shot across the screen.

Oops. Do-over. I started typing again.

A voice came from the bottom of the stairs. "Farley! Dinner's ready!"

"Okay, Mom. I'll be right down."

I quickly hit search and squinted at the illuminated screen. A bunch of ads for self-help books and energy drinks stared back at me. I was pretty sure I'd need a credit card for those, so no dice. Besides, I was also pretty sure drinking a Red Bull wasn't going to turn me into Burt. Just a very hyper version of Farley, if my experience with Mountain Dew and PEZ was anything to go by.

I kept reading, and that was when I saw it, all highlighted in a bright blue box, calling to me like the last *Dr. Fantastic* on the shelf at Grady's:

> *The Online Master's Guide to a Whole New You in Just Seven Simple Steps!*

A whole new you? Exactly what I was looking for! My palms began to tingle. This was perfect!

> *Tired of feeling invisible?*

Yes! Maybe a little too visible, really.

> *Tired of the world passing you by? Of everyone else getting the attention? The accolades? The life you deserve?*

Yes, yes, yes, and yes!

> *Then follow The Online Master's Seven Surefire Steps to Success!*

Seven steps. Just seven? That wasn't so bad. Like I said, I had exactly seven weeks till the new school year. So one step a week. Certainly doable. Heck, if I worked real hard, maybe I could pull 'em all off in seven days!

Plus, "A Whole New You" was written in super Day-Glo flashing red type, so it had to be good, right? I wiped my sweaty palms on my knees and clicked the blinking link.

In an instant the screen went dark and a giant head materialized—a giant head with flowy golden hair, big round eyes, and no body. Eek! I jolted backed in my chair.

"Aloha!" the giant head said in a robot voice that sounded weirdly like my old talking spaceman action figures. "I am The Online Master. And we are going to ride this wave together to a whole new you!"

Uh, okay . . .

"But first, fill in the blanks. . . ."

The head shrank into the upper left-hand corner, and a registration form filled the screen. I paused, sweat beading on the back of my neck. I'm not supposed to sign up for anything online, ever, without permission.

I inspected the form. I didn't see a spot for a credit card number, so that was cool. Besides, who said "Farley" actually had to be the guy doing the signing up, right?

I went to the name line, looked over my shoulder, and quickly typed, "Grover P. Quakenbush." A nervous chuckle slipped out of my mouth.

Date of birth: I decided to make Grover twenty-seven. That's pretty old.

E-mail address: why not grover@quakenbush.com? I imagined he'd be happy to get all my spam, whoever he was.

I clicked submit.

A little screen popped up, titled "Terms and Conditions." About a million words of tiny text followed. Whatever. Nobody ever reads that stuff, and I didn't have time anyway. I clicked accept, held my breath, and waited.

Suddenly, the screen went black and froze. My back stiffened. For a moment I wondered if the Internet cops were already preparing to kick down our front door and haul me off to the slammer for impersonating a made-up man. Was that a helicopter I'd just heard? I snuck a glance out my window and pulled the shades down. Maybe I should have read the fine print. . . .

But then The Online Master's tiny head appeared back in the corner of the screen.

"Aloha, Grover!" the head said.

Oh crud, here was my chance to be something cooler than Farley and I picked *Grover*? I wondered if I'd be stuck being Grover till the end of time.

"Today, Grover, your life changes forever!"

Apparently.

The Online Master smiled, and then—like magic— a row of fancy curled-up scrolls appeared on the screen, labeled steps one through seven. Now we were getting somewhere! I grabbed the mouse and moved the cursor over the first scroll. It lit up bright yellow and flashed. Awesome!

"Farrrrrrr-ley!" Mom yelled again in her hurry-up-I'm-not-waiting-anymore shriek. "Dinnnnnnn-errrrrr!"

Oh man. I needed to be fast. I clicked on the first step, and the scroll unfurled across the screen with a whooshing sound. *Cool!* Maybe self-improvement was going to be fun! The Online Master smiled in the corner and nodded in approval. So I began reading.

> *Step One: Your first objective is to envision your new self. If you can dream it, you can be it! So ask yourself: What do you want to be?*

Well, I thought, *if you must know, Batman*. He's got the coolest muscle suit and that Batmobile really rocks. But I was pretty sure that wasn't an option. I'd never fit in the suit. Plus, I can't drive. Or catch bad guys. Only thing I've ever caught was a bad case of chicken pox. Moving on, then.

> *Picture the real you that's yearning to break free. Remember, the most special thing about you comes from within. Now, focus on this new you, the exceptional you—the you that's been hidden beneath your layers of defenses!*

Wow. The Online Master was getting pretty personal. Could he see me or something? I sat up straight and smoothed out my shirt. Yeah, so I have plenty of layers.

But all right, I pictured a new Farley. A new and improved Farley. One who whacks baseballs clear over the fence and can actually make it all the way around the bases without collapsing midfield in a pile of dust. One who is witty and smart and makes people laugh—and not just because he can burp out the entire alphabet backward. One who Anna would be happy to meet again. And maybe—just maybe—one who made his dad proud, for once in his life.

That was the kind of Farley I wanted to be. The *better* kind.

I clicked on the next scroll. The first scroll rolled back up and disappeared in a shower of glittery gold stars, and the second unfurled. Cool!

> *Step Two: Let Go of the Old You*
> *To begin this exercise, draw a picture of you*
> *now—a picture of how you think the world*
> *sees you today. Be honest. Spare no detail.*
> *No matter how embarrassing.*

Ugh. *Drawing?* My heart sank just a little. I avoid art projects at all costs. And this was beginning to sound suspiciously like homework. Not exactly how I wanted to spend my summer break. Maybe I needed a different plan.

I hit the back button on my browser. The screen flashed. The words "There is no turning back on the path to enlightenment!" appeared and disappeared.

Step two popped back onto the screen.

I sighed and reclicked the back button.

> *There is no turning back on the path to enlightenment!*

I tried hitting the close window button.

> *There is no turning back on the path to enlightenment!*

I went to the menu and clicked exit.

> *There is no turning back on the path to enlightenment!*

What the heck?

"Farley!" Mom yelled. "What are you doing up there?"

"Just a minute, Mom," I shouted back. "Finishing a game!"

Click. Click. Click . . .

There is no turning back on the path to
enlightenment! There is no turning back
on the path to enlightenment! There is no
turning back on the path to enlightenment!

Fine! If I couldn't go back, I'd go forward. I slid the cursor across the screen and clicked the last scroll.

Nothing happened. But hey, at least I didn't get that stupid message. I clicked again.

Nada.

"Farley!!!" Mom yelled again. "Am I going to regret letting you have a computer in your room? I know how to check your history, you know! You'd better not be doing something you shouldn't."

Gah! Okay, one more try.

I jiggled the mouse and realigned the cursor. Sometimes with computers you just have to PRESS. REAL. HARD.

I gritted my teeth and pushed the mouse with all my might. *C'mon, c'mon, c'mon . . .* My entire arm vibrated with the pressure and my biceps quivered. And . . .

Zap!

"Ouch!" I shouted, yanking my hand back as a jolt of electricity shot through my pointer finger. There was a loud *pop*, and the computer screen went dark. The lights in my room flickered and dimmed. A strange whirring noise came from my hard drive, and the bulb in my desk lamp crackled ominously. The air smelled like my burnt shorts from camp, minus the fart.

Uh-oh.

My heart started to pound. Maybe I'd pushed a little too hard. . . . Oh man, Mom was going to kill me. This computer was supposed to last me until at least high school. (Or until I was a hundred if you asked Dad.)

"FARRRLEEEEY!" Mom shouted. "Now what are you doing? You'd better not be causing the power to surge!"

"Nope!" I squeaked, and wiggled the mouse, sweat beading on my forehead. "C'mon," I pleaded again. "C'mon!" (Because, hey, everybody also knows the best way to fix anything electronic is by talking to it.) "C'mon, c'mon, c'mon . . ."

Pop!

The screen flicked back to life and the roll of scrolls reappeared. A faint trail of—was that smoke and *gold glitter*?—twisted from somewhere behind my desk. Whatever. Enough was enough. The computer was working again and I wasn't going to hang around to witness if it blew up or something. Plausible deniability, as Dad calls it. Best not to be on the scene when the crime occurs.

"Farley!" Mom said.

"Yep, coming!" I reached out, pressed the computer power button and held it down until the screen went dark again, unplugged the thing—and got the heck out of there.

Bad move. Very bad move.

3

I HURRIED DOWNSTAIRS, SAT AT THE ROUND table in our hot, steamy kitchen, and wiped my forehead. No, our air-conditioning hadn't failed. It was just another mealtime in the Turner house. Let me explain: Mom doesn't cook. She boils. No one would ever accuse my mother of not knowing how to boil water. She's exceptional at it. It's all she does. Boiled eggs. Boiled beans. Boiled hot dogs. I bet you didn't know you can boil flank steak, did you? Well, you can't, actually. But that's never stopped Mom from trying.

"Here you go, honey." She slid a giant, steaming plate of spaghetti capped with a heap of dripping meatball sauce in front of me. A multigrain roll wobbled precariously alongside, a thick coat of that pretend butter Mom thinks is so delicious slathered on top.

I stared at my plate a moment, then at my oversize shirt. My stomach churned.

"Mom, pasta again?" I said. "Isn't it loaded with, uh, carts or something?"

"Carts?" Mom said. "Do you mean carbs?"

I shrugged, wishing I'd been paying more attention to that food pyramid thingy in health class.

Dad looked up wearily from his place at the table. He was all sweaty from the hot kitchen, navy blue tie loosened around his neck, white sleeves pushed up and shirt open at the collar. Dad spends his day driving one hour each way to the big city so he can win big cases for a big-city law firm and Provide for the Family. This makes him Very Tired. Mom spends her day doing graphic design work, Tending to Farley, and dreaming up new things to boil. This also makes her Very Tired.

My parents are experts at Tired.

Dad rubbed his weary face. "Geez, Farley. Carbs?" he said. "What are you talking about? You sound like you're middle-aged."

I squirmed a little in my chair. Dad would never understand what I was going through. He's basically perfect—class valedictorian, Harvard Law, broke the record for most consecutive strikeouts back in high school, et cetera, et cetera. You get the picture.

"Hey! I must object, Dave." Mom gave Dad a friendly slug on the arm. "I must object to that comment in defense of middle-aged people everywhere."

"Oh, I didn't mean you, hon. You're way too young to be middle-aged. Or to worry about carbs." He leaned over and kissed her steamed-pink cheek.

"Awww," she said.

Awww, barf.

I did my best to ignore that disgusting little love fest.

"Don't be silly, Far," Mom said. "You're a growing boy. You need your carbs."

No, what I needed was to squeeze into a Batman suit. Maybe I'd never made it past step one on my computer upstairs, but I knew if I had any chance of reinventing myself before the end of the summer, something had to give. And that something wasn't going to be the elastic in my pants.

So I thought about the fittest person I knew (besides Dad, of course). That would be Mr. Barnham, my PE teacher. He's always yammering on about CrossFit, dead lifts (which I hoped involved zombies!), and his special Paleo diet, which I think basically equals eating sticks and rocks and other caveman food. I looked at my plate. Squished tomatoes sounded pretty caveman-like, especially if they'd been pounded with a rock! I decided to focus on eating that.

"So, Farley," Dad said. "How was your day today?"

"Well," I said, covering my fork with sauce and licking it off. My tongue squished between the prongs in a desperate attempt to find a tomato molecule. "Burt and me went—"

"Burt and *I* went . . . ," Dad said.

"You went somewhere with Burt too?"

"Very funny, Farley. It's Burt and I. Burt and *I* went . . ."

"Okay, okay. Burt and *I* went to Grady's and got the newest issue of *Dr. Fantastic's Planet of Doom.* The one where Dr. Fantastic rescues the poor but noble Inickstrong people from inevitable destruction and saves them from the evil clutches of Lord Dracor. Except Lord Dracor escapes to the Glabow Galaxy. . . ."

Dad's eyes glazed over like the slick table surface.

"And after that we took a rocket ship into outer space and dug a tunnel to the center of the earth," I added. "We barely escaped being eaten by giant dinosaurs. But Burt shot them with his built-in laser beam just in time. His mom had it installed last year for Hanukkah."

"That's nice, Farley," Dad said. "So how was your day, hon?" He turned to Mom.

She started prattling on about the big lines at the grocery store, some client who wanted his logo in Comic Sans (which I gathered was bad, even though comics are

A-plus in my book!), and something she found spilled underneath the sofa that took her at least an hour to scrape away, which of course made her Very Tired. Dad countered her Tired argument with one of his own, involving stacks of endless paperwork, depositions, and expense reports for accounting. Whatever.

I returned to my futile sauce-extraction project. Maybe I could just lick the spaghetti and spit it back out. That would probably get me in trouble though. Plus, I might be tempted to take a bite. Or swallow it whole. I pushed the noodles aside and worked my way around a greasy meatball. No way was I touching one of those things. Cavemen definitely didn't have meatballs.

I scooped up some more tomato goo and my mind wandered to Anna. I wondered what she was doing. Unpacking? Having dinner too? Maybe she was sitting on top of a moving box, eating a crustless peanut butter sandwich with crunched-up potato chips sprinkled inside, her favorite food . . . No, scratch that. She probably ate much more sophisticated food now. Like that barely dead fish stuff rolled up in rice and seaweed. *Squishy*, I think.

"So, Farley," Dad said. "Have you selected your word of the day?"

"Huh?" I dropped my fork.

"Your *word*," Dad repeated.

"Yeah, right," I muttered. Every Wednesday Dad makes me choose a word I don't know from his giant million-year-old dictionary in the study and "exercise my brain" with it. For a while I tried choosing some really fun words. Like "derriere." That, in case you didn't know, is a fancy word for butt. (You're welcome.) Unfortunately, grown-ups don't seem to find it nearly as hilarious as other seven-year-olds, especially when you inform them (loudly) that you'll be sitting on yours to enjoy "story time." That wasn't a fun note from the teacher to take home in my backpack, by the way.

"Well?" Dad said.

"Imperative," I said.

"Good!" Dad nodded. "Definition?"

"Imperative, adjective meaning absolutely necessary or compelling," I recited.

"Excellent," Dad said. "Sentence?"

"Imperative," I droned on. "Is it imperative I complete these silly vocabulary lessons even during summer break?"

"Ha-ha. And the answer is yes. I didn't get where I am today by reading comic books all day long, you know," Dad said with a proud smile. Sure, okay. I'm pretty certain Dad was never actually a kid in the first place. It seems far more likely he was hatched fully grown, already outfitted in a boring blue suit and striped tie with a little flag pin attached.

"Okay, Dad." I pushed a few more noodles around my plate.

Finally, I'd sucked down as much sauce as humanly possible. I chugged my glass of milk and wiped away the little white mustache with my napkin. I was not raised in a barn, after all. I was only born next to one. Just ask Mom.

"May I be excused?" I said.

"Excused?" Mom said. "You've barely touched your dinner. Your mother worked very hard to make the family a nice meal tonight, you know."

I sighed. It's never a good sign for Farley when Mom starts referring to herself in the third person.

"I know, Mom. I'm just not hungry." Actually, I was hungry enough to eat my own arm. Which would probably make a mighty fine meal. But new and improved Farley wasn't a cannibal. Not yet, anyway.

"There's no dessert unless you eat your dinner," Dad warned.

"Maybe I could just have a rice cake later or something. Do we have any of those?"

"Rice cake, Farley?" Mom asked. "Are you feeling okay?" She suddenly sprouted that look like she was about to hustle over and test my forehead with the back of her hand or fetch the thermometer from the cabinet above the sink and jam it under my tongue.

"Honey? Are you all right?"

"Sure, Mom. I'm doing great!" Better than great, really. I was Batman in the making. Just without the cool car or suit. "Trying out this new Paleo thing, that's all. Eat like a caveman. Supposed to be good for you."

"Cavemen ate rice cakes?" Dad said.

I shrugged. "Aren't they kind of like rocks?"

Mom raised a skinny eyebrow and glanced at Dad.

"Okay, Farley, you may be excused," she said.

I cleared my place and headed back toward my room.

"Something's up with Farley," I overheard Mom say in a loud whisper as I creaked upstairs. I wrapped my fingers around the smooth wood railing, stopped, and listened. I know you shouldn't eavesdrop, but hey—sometimes it's the only way to find out what's going on around here. Especially if it involves yours truly.

"Up?" Dad said. His voice boomed and echoed through the tall foyer. I was pretty sure the fancy gold chandelier above me shook. Subtle, Dad's not. I think his head must always be in the courtroom, arguing cases.

"Yeah. He's acting kind of odd, don't you think?" Mom said. "He loves spaghetti, and now he wants to eat rocks?"

"He's an eleven-year-old boy," Dad answered. "They're *all* odd."

Hey, not eleven—eleven and three-quarters, thank you very much! Actually, I was eleven and eleven-twelfths if you wanted to be precise about the whole thing. My birthday was in five and a half weeks. Not that I was keeping track or anything.

"I don't know," Mom said. The water blasted on and dishes clanked in the sink. "I think he might have a crush. I may not have been an eleven-year-old boy before, but I recognize that goofy look."

"I suppose you do know your stuff, hon," Dad said. "Seen that look a million times on my face, haven't you?"

I rolled my eyes, glad I'd already made it to the top of the stairs so I didn't have to witness the inevitable kiss. It doesn't get much more disgusting than that. Or annoying. Because Mom was right, as usual.

Best to just retreat to my room, where it was safe.

But when I pushed open my door, a strange voice stopped me dead in my tracks with two simple words:

"Aloha, Grover."

4

WHAT?! I STOOD FROZEN IN MY DOORWAY AND peered nervously inside. I had to be imagining things. Because there was no way someone was talking to me. My eyes adjusted to the semi-darkness, and I could make out my bed, my dresser with the bottom drawer still open and underwear spilling out (nothing out of the ordinary there, phew), the piles of clothes all over the floor, my desk, and my compu—

I jumped back, stifling a scream.

"Aloha, Grover," the voice said again. My eyes followed the sound, landing on the slightly pixelated miniature man hovering above my monitor on what appeared to be a tiny surfboard. He was all of six inches high, wearing a flowy striped shirt-dress beach-coverup thingy. His wavy golden-blond hair lifted magically off his shoulders as if he were catching a wave—or being perpetually blown by an unseen fan, like a reality star on Instagram. His tanned bare feet dangled in front of the computer screen, which flickered an eerie green color.

"Ready to ride the wave to a whole new you?!" He made what I think was a hang-ten symbol and waggled his hand in the air.

I slammed my bedroom door shut, suddenly feeling extremely light-headed. Was this what happened when you abruptly deprived the body of carbs? Crazy hallucinations? (That would sure explain some of Mr. Barnham's random outbursts, like yelling at footballs to fly straight and pulling his own hair when basketballs didn't go through the net.)

I took a deep breath. Obviously I was just imagining things. Because there was no way a *miniature man* was sitting in my room, talking to me.

I exhaled and slowly creaked the door open again.

"First, you must put your toes in the water . . . ," the man began.

"Ahhhh!" I pinched my eyes shut. "*This isn't real. This isn't real. This isn't real*," I said over and over.

"What did you say, Far?" Mom shouted from downstairs. "You want some veal? I'm sorry. We don't have any. But if you eat your meatball you can have some pudding!"

"No. I don't want any veal!" I shouted back. I slipped into my room and closed the door, leaning heavily against it. The miniature man watched me with unblinking pixelated eyes. I watched him back, feeling even more freaked out than that time I got my head stuck in the staircase railing when I was four. At least when that happened, I got to meet a really cool fireman who gave me a plastic fire chief's hat once he'd extracted my noggin.

I inched my way closer to the *thing* on my computer.

"Who . . . ? I mean, *what* are you?" I said shakily. "And why are you in my room?"

"Dude, you don't remember me?" the tiny man said in his weird voice.

"Should I? Did I accidentally order you from the back of a comic book? Are you some sort of super-futuristic toy that got out of its box? Where's your plug?" I could feel my voice notching higher and higher.

"Ha-ha-ha, you're a funny dude," he said. "We just met, remember? I am The Online Master!"

"The Online Master?" I swallowed hard and shook my head. "You mean . . . ?" I pointed at the computer.

"Yes," he said. "The Online Master. But call me Tomy. Like Tommy, but with one *M*. I like to travel light."

"Tomy?"

"Heck yeah. It's an acronym. And a pretty righteous one, if I do say so myself. It's for T-O-M—"

"Sure . . . The Online Master," I broke in. "I get it. . . . But then what is the 'Y'?"

"Ah, right on." He nodded sagely. "The 'why.' You do understand."

A small laugh escaped my lips, and I glanced around the room. This had to be a trick. I wasn't sure how he was doing it, but it had to be Burt pranking me somehow. Hidden camera? *No, wait!* Maybe Burt was using that drone he got for his last birthday to beam a 3-D image through my window.

"Good one, Burt," I said with a nervous snort. I swatted at "Tomy's" image, expecting my hand to go straight through. Instead, it made contact, and the miniature surfer-guy fell onto my desk with a *thud*. He landed upside down, cover-up twisted around his head, tiny butt in the air. Ack! Why wasn't he wearing any pants?

I averted my eyes, unsure whether to laugh or to scream: I'd just been mooned by some freaky Internet . . . hoax? Hallucination? How was this even possible?

Tomy righted himself and raised a pair of tiny eyebrows at me. "Dude! Don't get all aggro on me."

"I'm sorry." I ran my eyes over his small body—

looking for a hidden off switch. "I didn't think you were real. Um, are you?"

"Ah, reality," Tomy said. "As Einstein was famously quoted on my Surf-N-Turf to-go cup, 'Reality is merely an illusion, albeit a very persistent one.'"

This guy was giving me a headache. A very persistent one. "That's not an answer. So, are you real, or not?"

"You can see me, right?" Tomy said.

"Sure." I gulped. "I can see you. But I don't know *why* I see you. . . ."

"Simple," Tomy said. "You manifested me."

"Mani-what?"

"Manifest."

"What does that even mean?" I said.

"Don't know what to tell you—only *you* know the true meaning, Grover," Tomy said.

I let out a loud sigh. "Can't you give me a straight answer? And can you call me something other than Grover. *Please?*"

"Sure. Like what?"

"I dunno." I shrugged. "How about Bruce Wayne?"

"Right on, Mr. Wayne," Tomy said. "The answer to your question is that *only you possess the answers within your-self.*" A satisfied smile crept across his face. "It took me a while to learn that one in Online Master orientation."

"C'mon, man." I squinted at him. "Stop speaking in riddles and tell me what you're doing here. Don't make me knock you down again!"

"Fine." He waved a tiny hand around. "You have manifested me into existence via your desire to create a new you—and, of course, by trying to skip ahead to the final step. You can't cheat the wave, my friend."

"Hey, I didn't cheat!" I said. "I was just trying to get off that page!"

"There are no shortcuts on the path to enlightenment," Tomy countered.

"So I've been told. But that still doesn't explain how you got out of there," I grumbled, pointing at my computer.

"Three clicks and a power surge," Tomy answered. "The magic combination. I'm kind of like a genie that way! Only better-looking, with more righteous hair." He laughed at his own silly joke.

My ears perked up.

"Wait, what? You're like a genie?"

"In a sense," Tomy answered.

"So, you can grant wishes?" I asked hopefully, rubbing my sweaty palms together. I mean, let's be real. I'm like pretty much every other kid on the planet—I'd been contemplating this moment ever since I watched *Aladdin* when I was five—right down to how I'd make my third and final wish. Which would be for infinite wishes, duh. If you don't do that, you're an idiot who doesn't deserve a genie. Transforming myself was going to be a *breeze*.

Tomy just looked at me and shook his head.

"No dice. The surfer rises to meet the wave, not the other way around. Besides, it's written in my code: I can grant you only that which you grant yourself." He bowed. And mooned me again.

Ugh. This had to be a nightmare. I just needed to go to bed. And when I woke up in the morning, this weird hallucination I was experiencing had better be gone.

The sun streamed through the edges of my blinds, birds sang outside, crickets chirped. Ah, the glory of a new day . . .

"Righteous morning, Mr. Wayne."

"Ack!" I screamed, jolting upright.

Tomy was not gone. Not at all.

Even worse, he was sitting at the end of my bed, staring at me with those big pixelated eyes. The morning sun glared off his golden hair, nearly blinding me. I pinched my eyes shut and pulled the covers to my chest.

I'm just dreaming. I'm just dreaming. . . .

I opened one eye.

"Good to see you on the dawn patrol. Ready to roll?"

"The what?" I sputtered, opening the other eye. "Why are you still here?"

"Ahhhh," he answered. "The existential mystery . . . Why are any of us here? Some say it's the call of the ocean. The pull of the tide . . ."

I groaned. "No, what do you want? Why don't you just get back in there?" I pointed at my computer across the room.

"Hmmm. That is not the question," Tomy said. "The question is what *you* want."

"What I want," I said, yanking the covers over my head, "is for you to go away."

I waited a moment, then peeked back out.

Tomy shook his head. "Sorry, dude," he said. "But I can't do that."

"What do you mean you can't?"

"I mean I can't. It's a word. It means the opposite of can." He nodded proudly.

"I know what it means. And I think you *can*."

"No," Tomy said. "I can't. Not until you've completed your journey."

"My journey?" I had no plans to go anywhere today. Well, other than Josh's pool.

"The one you began last night." Tomy pointed at my

computer. Scrolls one through seven were lined up across the top of the screen. Scrolls two through seven blinked ominously.

"I don't know," I said. "I think I might've changed my mind. I wasn't aware that whole project came with . . . well, *you*. Mom won't even let me have a goldfish. She's not going to approve of me having a pet—I don't know—genie thing, or whatever you are. I'll just tackle this on my own, thanks."

"Oh hey, chill, little dude," Tomy said. "It's all about the good vibes, positive thinking. I'm here to help!"

"Well, I think I'm just going to put you back in the computer, if it's all the same," I said. I got up and walked across the room, ignoring Tomy, and held the computer's power button down until the screen went black. The room went silent. No whir of the computer fan, no crackle of electricity—I glanced over my shoulder—and ha, no Tomy!

Whew! "That was easy," I said, wishing every annoying thing in my life came with an off switch. Pre-algebra would be a snap!

"Sure, dude," a voice answered. "But was it truly?"

"What?" I shrieked, nearly falling backward onto my butt.

The computer in front of me lit up again, and the

scrolls flashed back across the top of the screen. Tomy was now perched on the monitor, surfboard in hand, swinging his bare feet and nodding his golden curls. I considered running and getting my mom, but I stopped myself. If she thought the sea monkeys were bad, what would she have to say about *this*?

"What is going on?" I said, voice rising a notch. "This seriously can't be happening."

I held the power button down again, staring at Tomy the entire time. He stared right back. I pushed harder on the button, till my finger turned purple.

But the scrolls kept flashing.

The screen stayed lit.

And Tomy stayed put.

"Why isn't this working?" I said in exasperation.

"Ah," Tomy said with a slow head nod. "Maybe it is."

He turned and glanced behind the computer.

I followed his gaze—down the back of my desk, along the wall, and to the computer's power cord—which was dangling, completely detached from the outlet, right where I, Farley Andrew Turner, aka Grover Quackenbush, aka Bruce Wayne—had left it unplugged the night before.

(At this point I really did fall onto my butt, and I don't know—maybe passed out in shock. The only thing

I really remember is coming to on the floor, muttering to myself, neck sweating.)

"This isn't possible," I said, rubbing my eyes.

"Anything is possible," Tomy said with a wave of his suntanned hand, "when you follow the path to enlightenment. Especially if it leads to Zuma Beach!"

He tapped the second flashing scroll with his bare foot.

I looked at Tomy. I looked at the unplugged cord. I looked back at Tomy, who nodded again. "You agreed to the terms and conditions," he said. "Once you're in the wave, you're committed to the ride."

Well, judge all you want. But what choice did I have? I *knew* I should've read that fine print. . . .

Besides, love, as my uncle Ron says (and he's been married, like, four times, so he's something of an expert), will make you do crazy things. Crazy, ridiculous, *embarrassing* things.

Which is why—I now know—love is sort of like the Internet.

Best avoided.

5

I PLUNKED MYSELF IN MY CHAIR. THE SECOND scroll reappeared.

> *Step Two: Let Go of the Old You*
> *To begin this exercise, draw a picture of you*
> *now—a picture of how you think the world*
> *sees you today. Be honest. Spare no detail.*
> *No matter how embarrassing.*

I pulled a piece of crumpled scrap paper from my drawer, flattened it out on the desk, and started drawing. Tomy stared at me the entire time. I hoped this didn't take long. I needed to be at Josh's by ten.

My pencil scraped across the paper: one milk chocolate coin for a head. A big doughnut for a body. A couple of stuffed sausages for legs and arms. Biscuit hands and feet. Licorice hair. Matching gumdrop eyes. Candy dot for a nose. And a Pixy Stix mouth.

My stomach growled. I hadn't eaten breakfast yet. And that sauce dinner wasn't exactly holding me over.

I shoved the picture aside, turned back to the computer screen, and took a bite of my pencil.

Now, take this picture of the old you,
crumple it up, and throw it away.

Boom. Done.

"Excellent. The most difficult thing is to release your old self. That and mastering the Rodeo Flip. *Cowabunga!*" Tomy struck a surf pose, knees bent, arms out.

"Humph," I mumbled, returning to my assignment. Something told me that was hardly the most difficult part.

Now you are ready to begin the new you!
On a new piece of paper, draw the new you.
The one you envision. The one waiting to
break free from inside the old you!

All right. I grabbed a new paper and started drawing. Still a coin head (though I'll admit, for a moment I considered going trapezoid, just for kicks. But no, at the rate things were going I might have "manifested" one into existence and I'd never fit in another hat again.)

I drew myself a solid rectangle body. Hockey sticks for legs and baseball-bat arms. Powerful bats. The kind that make a colossal cracking sound when they hit the ball. Then I put some brown hair on top. Cool hair. Not the tangled knot I currently sport, but the good kind of messy, like the guys on the Disney Channel. I added eyes. A nose. Mouth. Oh, and ears. I was pretty sure I'd forgotten ears on Old Farley. Didn't matter, though. He was in the metal trash can under my desk. New Farley had ears. Nice ears. Not the type that stuck out like two open car doors flopping in the wind.

I shook New Farley in the air and inspected my handiwork.

"Satisfied?" I asked Tomy. "Can we move on now?"

In typical Tomy fashion, he answered in a nonanswer.

"The question is: Are you satisfied?"

To be honest, I wasn't. Something was missing. And no, it wasn't the Bat Suit. New Farley was just a little too . . . ordinary. How could this guy be the hero of his own story?

I rolled the pencil between my fingers and thought.

If New Farley could be anything . . . *anything* . . . what would he be?

I glanced around my room and inspected the *Dr. Fantastic* poster taped above my desk . . . the solar system swirling over my bed . . . the little glowing stars glued to the ceiling.

Inspiration struck like a bad burrito.

I quickly flipped over my pencil and sketched a round space helmet on New Farley. Then I put a matching suit on his body. For good measure, I drew Mars and Venus hovering in the background and the ruddy surface of the moon beneath New Farley's brand-spanking-new gravity boots. And the finishing touch: a few stars sprinkled around New Farley's head and a comet blasting through the sky.

"*Ta-da!*" I said.

Tomy nodded in approval, so I kept reading.

> *Next, take this picture of the new you and*
> *hang it somewhere you'll see it every day.*
> *Look at it every day! Remind yourself,*
> *this is the person you are inside! This is the*
> *person you aim to be!*

I found a piece of tape and stuck New Farley to the side of my computer monitor. I stared at it till my eyes went blurry and New Farley turned into a swirl of pencil squiggles. I wondered how long this was supposed to take.

(Spoiler alert: forever.)

But hey, how was I to know better?

I turned back to the computer, avoiding eye contact with the weird little dude sitting on top of it:

> *Finally, go to a peaceful place, one where you*
> *will not be disturbed and can properly focus.*
> *In this place, you should sit and meditate on*
> *the new you. Close your eyes. Breathe slowly*
> *and release the old you as you exhale. Feel*
> *the old you slip away with every breath! Feel*
> *your potential inside growing and expanding*
> *each time you inhale!*

"Seriously?" I said.

Tomy crossed his legs, pressed his palms together above his head, closed his eyes, and exhaled loudly.

"Ahhhhh!" he said.

I left Tomy in my room and slipped past Mom, who was in front of her computer in the office muttering, "Comic Sans, Comic Sans . . . not a font, an abomination!" and walked out our back door. I figured the yard was the most peaceful place we had around here. Well, besides the bathroom. That's where Dad goes to do all his thinking.

I had a look around: patio, table and chairs, a bunch of neatly mown grass, and that fort Dad had started building about a hundred years ago and never finished. All nice enough, but I needed peaceful. Extra peaceful if I was going to wipe out Old Farley in one sitting and make that annoying pest in my room go away.

Ooh! I had an idea!

I plodded across the yard to Mom's "relaxation garden" by the back fence. Mom saw this ad in a catalog a few years back for this little tray of sand you stick on your desk and scrape with a tiny rake to make soothing swirly patterns. She wanted it really bad, but she couldn't bring herself to pay $39.95 for a tin full of sand. So instead, she took my old green plastic turtle sandbox, filled it with dirt, and bought a miniature garden rake for seventy-five cents at a yard sale—and whammo! Instant calm.

She was pretty pleased with herself too. After all, why go for just a little relaxation when you can have a lot, right? It was too bad for New Farley I usually have the same reaction when it comes to cake.

I stopped at the edge of the turtle's cracked green plastic head. Mom's rake was dropped on top, rusted in place. A set of cat footprints ran straight across the middle of the unswirled dirt, which was covered in dead leaves and twigs. I pushed the rake and debris aside and looked over my shoulder to make sure no one was watching.

Oh well, here went nothing.

I climbed into the center, sat down, crossed my legs like Tomy, and put my hands on my knees. Squishy dirt collected around the tops of my socks. I wondered if I needed to chant. Probably, right?

Ohm . . . ohm . . . ohm . . .

Forget it. I wasn't chanting.

Instead, I closed my eyes and tilted my face toward the warm sun.

Breathe in, New Farley. Breathe out, Old Farley. In, out. In, out.

Deep breaths. Cleansing breaths. My muscles loosened and my breathing slowed.

Ahhh, this actually was sort of relaxing. Maybe I'd even make Mom a nice little swirly pattern when I was done. For inspiration. I wiggled a little and my butt sank deeper into the soft dirt. Little granules worked their way under my shorts and collected around my underpants.

Now, I suppose at this point you're probably wondering why on earth I was sitting in a pile of dirt so I could try to impress a girl I had a crush on back when I was six. One I hadn't seen in five years. One who might not even remember me in the first place. And it's a valid question. One I've admittedly been asking myself a lot recently.

But here's the thing—I was actually kind of counting on Anna not remembering me. Because for once I had a chance to be someone else. I'd known everyone here in Middleford—from Burt to the guy who rings up comics at Grady's—for pretty much my whole life. And no matter what I did, no matter how much I changed, no one at MMS, Home of the Flying Squirrels, would ever see me any differently.

But Anna might.

And then, if I was lucky—maybe everyone else would too.

Including Dad.

I took another deep breath.

In, New Farley. Out, old. In, out. In, out.

Birds chirped happily in the trees, leaves rustled in the warm summer breeze, gentle wings fluttered . . . *in, out, in, out* . . . Old Farley began to slip away. *There he goes. He's almost gone . . .* and . . .

Splat!

I reached up and wiped the bird poop from my forehead.

Things were not getting off to a good start.

6

I LUMBERED BACK TO MY ROOM, RUBBING THE poop from my hair with a dish towel.

"Eww, gnarly, dude," Tomy said. "What happened to you?"

"You don't want to know."

"Right on," Tomy said. "Good news, though! You have conquered the second step! See?"

He tapped the screen, and the second scroll rolled back up tight with a fantastic *whoosh*. A shower of gold glitter burst from above the computer and rained over Tomy's head.

"Whoa."

"Awesome, yeah?"

"Not bad," I said. "But I've got to clean up and get out of here."

Tomy leapt to his tiny feet and smoothed out his beach-dress. "Excellent! Where are we going? A jam? Fire pit on the beach? Should I change my threads?"

"*We* are not going anywhere," I answered. "You can leave your threads right where they are. *I* am going to Josh's pool."

"A pool!" Tomy exclaimed. "Duuuuude, you have to let me ride shotgun!" He tucked his surfboard under his arm. "It's been too long since I've caught a wave."

"Nope."

Tomy's lower lip formed a pixelated pout.

"Then can you point me in the direction of the nearest beach?"

"For starters, we're in the middle of Massachusetts. There are no beaches!" I said. "Besides, you can't leave my room. Understand? *No one can see you.* Not Josh. Not Burt. And *especially* not my parents. Got it?"

"But you can see me."

"I wish I couldn't." I grabbed my pool stuff, headed toward my bedroom door, and glanced over my shoulder. "Just *stay in here*, understood? Do. Not. Go. Anywhere. And whatever you do, if anyone comes in, hide!"

Tomy bowed his head and said in a faux-deep voice, "Your wish is my command, Master Wayne." He grinned. "A wish, get it? That is rad genie humor, yeah?"

I rolled my eyes and walked into the hall. "Just stay put," I said, closing the door behind me. "And don't get me into any trouble!"

Josh, Burt, and I sat around the Chans' patio table, chilling next to the pool, and I tried to forget about Tomy. The patio door slid open. Mr. Chan strolled out, flip-flops flapping, a bottle of Sprite tucked under his arm and paper cups in hand.

"Hello, boys!" he said in his chipper singsong voice. Mrs. Chan earns, like, a bazillion dollars as a financial advisor, and Mr. Chan's job is to take care of Josh, his three sisters, and their cat, Sprinkles. He's pretty cool, and thanks to him we've never missed the newest Marvel movie.

"I thought you boys might like some soda." Mr. Chan dropped the bottle and cups on the table next to Burt.

"Burt, my man!" he said, raising his fist. "Pound dog!"

Burt fist-bumped him. "Yo, Mr. C."

"Farrrrr-leeeeeey," Mr. Chan said next, striking a pose that I think was supposed to be the Incredible Hulk flexing his muscles. Or he was trying to pass gas. I'm not sure. He does it every time he sees me, and I still haven't figured it out.

"Hi, Mr. Chan," I said with a little salute.

Josh nodded. "'Kay, thanks, Dad."

"You're welcome," he said, heading back inside. "Have fun, and don't scare the cat! Last time you boys raised a ruckus out here, we found her half a mile away, hiding in the Duggans' garbage bin! Took a whole can of tuna to bribe her out."

"Got it, Dad," Josh said.

The sliding door *whoosh*ed shut. Josh twisted the green cap from the soda bottle, and a hiss of air escaped the top. Then he sloshed some of the fizzing liquid in our cups. We each picked one up and waited, drinks raised, as is customary in our solemn ritual.

Josh nodded. Burt nodded in response. I executed a slight tip of the head. It suddenly occurred to me this was probably not appropriate behavior for New Farley. In fact, if New Farley expected to be taken seriously, he needed to act in a much more dignified manner. Like . . . Dad.

I cleared my throat and tried to remember his annual New Year's toast. "As you slide down the banister of life," I said, "may the splinters always be pointed so they're not poking you in the butt." I cleared my throat again and smiled. That wasn't too shabby, if I did say so myself.

I had a fleeting image of New Farley at the podium at middle school graduation, his eloquent yet touching speech inspiring the crowd, bringing tears to his mom's eyes and his dad to his feet, applauding loudly. *That's my son! My! Son!*

Burt and Josh shot me blank stares.

"Sure, Farley," Josh said. "Hold on to your butt, or whatever. Now . . . go!" We all chugged our drinks as fast as possible. Tingles of fizz tickled my nose. I held in a sneeze. My eyes watered.

Buurrrp went Burt.

Buuuuurrrppp went Josh.

They wiped their mouths and looked expectantly at me, holding in my cheeks. Josh smiled. Burt nodded his head up and down in anticipation.

Oh, what the heck. Might as well send Old Farley out with a bang.

I breathed in through my nose. *Breath in, New Farley. Breath out . . .*

BUUUUUUUUUUURRRRRRRRRPPPPPPPPPP!!!

The table rattled. Sprinkles darted behind a bush. Mr. Chan pulled the kitchen window shut, and a neighborhood dog howled.

Burt and Josh doubled over laughing.

"Don't pee your pants, Squirt," Josh said, clutching his side.

Burt choked on his soda. "Fartley, that was awesome," he said, coughing.

"That may be his best one yet! He even made Sprite come out my nose with that one!" Josh wiped his face with the back of his hand and pointed in my direction.

"Fartley, you're awesome," Burt said.

"Thank you," I said, and let out an appreciative burp.

"You're killing me!" Josh said, clutching his belly. "Stop it!"

Burp, burp, burp.

Say good-bye, Old Farley. You had a nice run. I shook my head and gave Old Farley his final word.

Buuuuurp!

And with that I ran and did a huge cannonball into the pool. Burt and Josh dove in immediately after.

"Race you, Squirt," Josh hollered. They both took off in a massive kick of chlorinated water, not even bothering to challenge me. I couldn't blame them, though. What was the point?

But the truth was, at that moment I didn't mind. I leaned back, face up toward the bright sun, points of light filtering through my closed eyelids. I let the water go all the way up over my ears so every sound was muted, Burt and Josh's *whoops* and yells a million miles away as they battled each other in headstand and somersault competitions.

The pool may be one of my favorite places on earth.

Here I was weightless. Floating. Bobbing in the water. In the pool I was Astronaut Farley, tumbling through space, free from the pull of gravity.

Had I known what was waiting for me in my room when I got home, I wouldn't have been nearly as relaxed.

7

MOM PICKED ME UP LATER THAT AFTERNOON on her way back from spin class. (Side note: In case you weren't aware, spin class is where a bunch of people ride stationary bikes along to music while some person up front wearing spandex and a headset shouts "encouragement" at them. I know. I was also disappointed to discover it didn't involve a bunch of people spinning around a room like out-of-control tops. My preschool years would've been a lot more fun.)

"Hi, Mom." I slid into the back of the minivan and closed the door. (Yes, Mom still makes me ride in the back. Safest place in the car, according to her. Lucky for me, I got too wide for my booster seat about five million years ago.)

"Hi, Farley. How was Josh's?" Mom asked.

"Good," I said.

"Hmmm," Mom answered, clicking her nails on the steering wheel and glancing back at me in the rear-view mirror as we pulled onto the road. "Just good? Anything else?"

"It was great?" I said, trying to figure out where this was headed. Every time Mom gets that sweetly inquisitive tone, I can be sure she's attempting to ferret some sort of information out of me without actually asking. Like whether I was the one who hid boiled lima beans beneath the dining room flower arrangement. Spoiler alert: none of your business.

"Hmmm," she said again. A few moments of silence. This was the part where I knew she expected me to volunteer something. But I wasn't stupid. I'd learned my lesson that time I copped to setting all the clocks in our house back an hour so I'd miss going to my cousin's birthday party. (I mean, the kid was turning three and the party was in a bounce house with a bunch of other not-fully-potty-trained three-year-olds hopped up on cotton candy. Can you really blame me?!)

"Oh, I got you a few things from your list of, uh, cave-man food," Mom continued. "Ran it by Dr. Fiorenza to make sure it was okay. Everything in moderation, buddy, as long as . . ."

Mom kept talking about healthy choices, not diets, blah-blah, as we turned down Burt and Anna's street, but I'd stopped listening. The only thing I heard was the distant sound of a basketball bouncing. . . . *Thump, thUMP, THUMP!* It grew louder. And louder . . . And there was the telltale red hair. Oh no!

I couldn't let her see me yet!

I quickly flung myself sideways, pressing my body flat onto the bottom of the seat. My head hit the armrest on the way down. My underpants gave me an insta-wedgie.

"Oof," I said, trying not to hyperventilate—or move. Who knew how far up my belly protruded when I inhaled?

"Farley?" Mom said. "Are you okay back there? Where did you go?"

"I'm fine," I said. "Just dropped my banana."

"You brought a banana back from Josh's?"

I slapped my forehead. I didn't have a banana. Why did I even say that?

"I meant bandana," I said. "I dropped my bandana."

I grimaced. What was the matter with me? I didn't have one of those, either.

The sound of the basketball bouncing grew louder. Mom suddenly tapped the brakes and drove slower. "Huh . . . ," she mumbled. "Interesting." My heart pounded.

Don't stop, Mom. Don't stop!

Thankfully, Mom pressed the accelerator and didn't say another word. I stayed flat to the seat and listened until the bouncing faded away—then slowly sat back up and rubbed my head (and extracted my stuck underpants). Mom stayed silent up front as we pulled into our driveway. She clicked off the ignition. Then she just sat there, *still* being weirdly quiet. She turned and smiled at me. A little *too* Mom-friendly-like . . .

"You *sure* you don't have anything on your mind . . . ?"

"Noooo . . . Is there something on *your* mind?" I said, the back of my neck inexplicably starting to sweat. I began to make a mental list of the things I might have done and how I might deny them. I mean, Dad hates lima beans too. . . .

"Oh, no," Mom said a bit too brightly. "Everything is fine. I was just taking some laundry to your room this afternoon and . . ."

"What?" The sweat on my neck turned cold. My spine stiffened. "My room?" I said with a gulp.

"Yeah, honey," Mom said. "Don't look so alarmed. I was just surprised, that's all. Not what I was expecting to find when I opened your door. I mean, not that I . . ."

But I didn't hear the rest of what Mom said because I'd already leapt from the car, bolted into the house, and taken the stairs five at a time—okay, I'm exaggerating a bit; I took them one at a time, but I went fast . . . ish, okay?!—and flung open the door to my room.

My hand flew over my mouth.

"What have you done?" I whispered. No wonder Mom was acting so weird. There was absolutely no way I could explain this. . . .

"You dig it?" Tomy's voice answered. He peeked around the computer.

"I, uh, sure. It's just . . . ," I started. I heard the front door open and Mom walk inside.

"Farley," Mom shouted up the stairs.

"Yeah?" I squeaked.

"I just wanted to say thank you," she said. "Whatever your reasons, I appreciate it, okay?"

"Okay, Mom," I answered, looking around my spotless room. Yes, I said *spotless*. The bed was made, the windows sparkled, and I could actually see my carpet. I didn't even remember that it was light blue. Huh. All of my books and papers were carefully organized on my desk, pencils arranged in a cup. The dresser drawers were closed, and when I pulled one open, all of my underpants were folded neatly inside and lined up in a row next to my carefully rolled socks.

"You cleaned my room?" I said to Tomy.

He smiled and nodded. "Easier to focus. Like when you're the first one to the beach and it's just you and the ocean. Nothing to distract you . . ." He stared wistfully toward the ceiling.

Okay. Whatever that meant. I didn't care. For a brief, fleeting moment, I thought it might actually be good to have Tomy around.

Of course, at that point, I hadn't clicked on the next scroll.

Step Three: Chart the Journey
Now you've envisioned the new you.
But how do you reach your goals? You
wouldn't head out on a trip without a
navigation system, or at least a map,
would you?

I guessed not. But then, I'd never really gone much farther than the ten blocks to Burt's house. And the two miles to school. And Josh's pool, of course. Mom and Dad drive me everywhere I go. I'm not permitted past the end of our driveway without supervision. After all, you can't be too safe. At least that's what Mom has determined watching CNN every night.

So, you must chart a path to the new you!
You have your picture. Now write down
the main characteristics of this new and
improved self. List at least three.

Tomy handed me a piece of scrap paper from the pile he'd carefully arranged on my desk, along with a pencil. I bit the metal tip and flattened it with my teeth, thinking.

Okay, three characteristics of New Farley, the great and fearless space explorer:

1.   Sleek and muscular (I had to fit in an astronaut suit, after all).
2.   Smart.

I chewed harder on the pencil. What else were astronauts, besides the coolest people on the planet? Scratch, that—the galaxy. Oooh . . . I knew!

3.   Brave.

I gave myself a little pat on the back. That wasn't so bad. I was cruising through these steps. Tomy would be gone and I'd be a changed man before I knew it. Next!

Now think about what you need to do
to reach your goals. For example, if you
want more friends, meet more people.
Contemplate your goals and write at least
one way you can reach each.

I flipped over the paper and scratched out another list.

1. Eat like a caveman and exercise.

I paused a moment. Probably it would be wise to get rid of the emergency Twinkies I kept under my bed if I have a bad day. Just in case. I was sure New Farley wouldn't need them. And cavemen definitely didn't eat those. I walked over, grabbed the box, and shoved my hand inside. My fingers crinkled the plastic wrappers as I counted. Seven left. Instinctively, my mouth watered. Soft yellow cake. Smooshy cream filling. *Will. Not. Give. In.*

Will not!

I stared at the box. Maybe I wouldn't throw them out. Maybe I'd just stick them on my nightstand like Grandpa Andrew did with his old cigarettes. According to Grandpa, he quit smoking way back in the 1800s or something. But he kept those dusty old smokes just to remind himself who's boss.

I gingerly set my Twinkie box in a place of honor next to the bed, returned to my desk, and got back to work on my list.

Okay, *smart*?

That was tougher. Summer was when I generally shut my brain off, so it could rest up for long division once school started.

I held my pencil in the air and glanced at Tomy, who had taken up residence on my mouse pad and was using it as a yoga mat.

"Remember," he said, lying flat on his stomach and tilting his head up and back till it almost touched his feet. *How does he do that?* His voice squeaked. "You mustn't nourish only the body—you must also nourish the soul."

"Can I feed it a rock?" I asked.

Tomy shook his head.

Okay, then. How was I supposed to nourish my soul? I wasn't even sure where it was located. Probably somewhere gross. Like my big toe.

Ooh, wait! I had it! Mom has all these books called *Chicken Nuggets for the Soul*, or something like that. So, that's what I would do. I'd read! How hard could that be? I mean, I blow through *Dr. Fantastic*s like nobody's business. Except for this, I needed to read something more important. Really important.

Like the most important book in the world! That would make me extra smart. And in one sitting, too!

I opened a new window and searched. Well, would you look at that! Right there on my screen was a list of the most important books in history. The Bible was first. No thanks. I got enough of that in Sunday school. Then there were a bunch of things with names I couldn't pronounce. But wait! There was one called *War and Peace*.

That sounded good, especially the war part. Hopefully there would be a lot of intergalactic battles.

2. Read *War and Peace*.

But for the last characteristic—brave? That was going to be tricky. Because there was only one way to demonstrate bravery, and it was the hardest thing of all:

3. Do something heroic.

> *Now, put this list alongside your drawing*
> *of the new you. This is your guidepost as*
> *you complete the next steps! Refer to it often*
> *and adjust as needed. The new you is in a*
> *glorious state of evolution!*

I taped my list next to New Astronaut Farley and looked at Tomy.

"Yeah?" I said.

A poof of glittery gold erupted and rained down over his head as scroll three snapped shut.

"Heck yeah!" He nodded and gave me a tiny fist bump.

I figured I'd better get started, so I lumbered into the family room in search of some exercise. I was pretty sure Mom had a whole bunch of old workout DVDs stashed away somewhere. I opened the cabinet under the television and peered inside, past Mom's "sewing club" box, which is basically a pile of random fabric scraps, thread, and needles. The last Thursday of every month all the neighborhood ladies come over to "sew." Only Dad says it's just an excuse to get together, drink wine, and complain how Very Tired they are. Judging from the two half-stitched quilt squares in here with untied threads hanging off the sides, my guess was Dad's right.

I shoved that junk to the side and kept searching.

"Ugh. Where are they?" I muttered.

"Perhaps what you seek is already inside you," a voice whispered into my ear.

I nearly had a heart attack on the spot. "What the . . . ?"

I glanced over my shoulder. A pixelated head popped out of my hoodie and nodded at me.

"You!" I said. "You scared me half to death! What are you doing in there?"

"Just making dinner!" Mom shouted from the kitchen. A couple of pots and pans rattled, and the water blasted on.

"It's okay. I'm fine!" I hollered back. I glared at Tomy. He smiled. "Just keep it down," I said. "And don't let anyone see you!"

His little head popped back inside my hoodie. I reached farther into the cabinet.

Aha! There behind an old CD player were Mom's exercise videos in a lopsided stack covered with dust. I removed the first one called *Fat Burner!* It had a picture on the front of a skinny lady in purple tights and a silver bodysuit with big poufy hair like Mom's old high school photo. Fat-burner lady was turned sideways in a funny pose with her knees bent, arms up, and butt poking out like she was farting or trying real hard to poop. Three smiling helmet-haired ladies behind her did the same dumb fart-poop pose.

Maybe exercise was going to be fun!

I pulled out the DVD and popped it in the player. In moments, Fart Lady from the front cover yelled in a super-loud, squeaky voice, "Let's get in shape today!"

She clapped her hands three times and started marching. "Let's go. One! Two! Three!"

I stood in front of the TV and lifted my knees up and down like the ladies on the screen. My oversize shorts puffed out like parade balloons.

"Very good!" Fart Lady yelled. "Now, arms up and to the sides."

She started flapping like she was preparing for blast-off. I did the same. Only I stayed stuck on the ground. Shocking, I know.

"Foot to the front!" she ordered. "Lunge! Lunge! Reach for your toes!"

I stomped forward with my left foot, then my right. I started breathing heavy. The framed photo of baby Farley in the cow suit rattled on the wall above the fireplace.

Keep it moooo-ving!

Tomy bounced up and down in my hood. *Oof. Aye. Cowabunga!*

All of Dad's baseball trophies shook in the bookshelf. Little gold bats twitched at invisible pitches. Dad must have a hundred awards in there, all from the days when you actually had to win the game in order to get a prize (as he's fond of pointing out). They crowded out the one flimsy certificate I scored for "participation" when I was six, the only season I played Little League. Back then

Dad had grand visions of young Farley following in his athletic-scholarship footsteps.

But Dad's big Farley-the-athlete dreams were dashed right about the fifth time I was beaned in the nose with a ball. I think that's when he finally realized all those emergency room visits were going to cost way more than tuition. (That's also about the time I realized the best way to deal with crushing disappointment—and getting beaned with a ball—was to shout *bazoinga!* and fall sideways in the dirt dramatically like a cartoon character. Bonus points for throwing in zombie arms.)

"And twist! Twist!"

I turned left and right. I wiped sweat from my forehead and licked my lips. They tasted like salt. I focused hard to keep from thinking about popcorn balls.

"Great!" yelled Fart Lady. She propped her hands on her hips and marched. "Now we're all warmed up! Time to burn some calories!"

What? We were just *warming up*?

"Lift your arms, left and right and lunge, lunge!"

I groaned. I was getting ready to die here. Gasp . . . for . . . air!

Footsteps approached. Too . . . tired . . . to . . . look.

"Farley, what on earth are you doing?"

I jumped. Well, sort of. Something in me jumped,

maybe my spleen. Dad stood behind me on the family-room steps, black leather briefcase in his left hand, a mystified look on his overworked face.

"Geez, Farley, first carbs and now *aerobics*?" He loosened that boring blue tie and rubbed his head. His black hair stuck up in seventy-five different directions. I waited for him to shout, "I object!" He glanced past my head, eyebrow raised. Tomy twitched against my back. Nervously, I yanked the drawstrings on my hood, closing him inside.

Dad lowered his eyebrow. "What has gotten into you?"

I didn't expect Dad, with his caseful of trophies, to even remotely understand. So I spoke in language he would get.

"I'm just," I panted. "I'm just . . . trying." *Breathe, Farley, breathe!* "I'm just trying to get some . . . exercise, cool?"

Dad walked over to the television and turned it off.

"Oh yeah?" he said. "You want to get some exercise?"

I nodded. I couldn't breathe anymore.

"That's great! You can come running with me! Every morning. Crack of dawn! Forget this." He made a yuck face like he'd just bitten a sour lemon and shook his finger at the fart-lady box on the floor. *Bad, Fart Lady. Order in the court! Bailiff, take her away!* "How does that sound?" he asked.

I panted a couple of times. It was hard to imagine this would turn out any better than that horrible Season of Spring Training when I was six. Ten push-ups every morning. Ten sit-ups every night. Ten million too many trips to the batting cage. During which I'm pretty sure I never hit a single pitch. And I really tried. But I was always swinging too early, or too late, or just not swinging at all (judging by Dad's continuous over-my-shoulder "help").

All that was bad enough. But the look on Dad's face every time I struck out was even worse. He tried to hide it, but I could see what he was thinking after every swing: that his son was a failure.

That familiar sensation crept over me—the one where my stomach gets all queazy and my ears begin to ring. This was right about the time Old Farley would let one rip for comedic effect and make a break for it. New Farley, though . . .

"Okay?" Dad said again.

"Sure, Dad," I puffed out, and forced a smile. "Sounds good."

"Good!" he said. "Tomorrow morning. Bright and early! We'll do this right, partner!"

I'm pretty sure at that point I passed out on the floor.

9

"BUM-BA-DA-DUM-DA-DA-DUM-DI-DEE-DUM," DAD sang. "*Bum-ba-da-dum-da-da-dum-di-dee-dum.*" His voice started getting louder and his feet did a weird little dance-shuffle on the sidewalk. "*Da-da-daaaah . . .*"

"What is that, Dad?"

"Huh?" He stopped singing.

"That," I said. "The song. That *thing* you're doing."

"Oh, *Rocky*. Theme song from *Rocky*. *Bum-ba-da . . .*"

"*Rocky?*"

"Yeah, *Rocky*. Running up the steps of the Philadelphia Museum of Art." He jabbed at the air with balled-up fists and did the little dance again. "Pow-pow! Ka-pow! KO!"

I started to think maybe that sweatband was squeezing Dad's head too hard. Or he'd lost his mind. Or both. I waited for the dance-boxing to stop. Dad glanced sideways at me, standing there in my matching headband and spandex running shorts. Dad let me borrow a pair of his shorts. He's about two feet taller than me, but I'm two feet wider, so they worked out all right since they're made of some super-futuristic stretchy material. I had my own giant *Dr. Fantastic* shirt over them. Fortunately (or unfortunately, depending on how you look at things), there was no place for a stowaway Online Master to hide—so Tomy was back in my room. Doing heaven knew what.

"So, this Rocky guy?" I asked. "Does he morph or something?"

"Huh?" Dad said.

"Does he morph into a rock? Is that why he's called Rocky?"

"No, Far. He's a fighter." *Bam-bam.* Dad punched the helpless air.

"Does he have superpowers, then?"

"No, Far. No superpowers."

"Does he at least blow stuff up?" I asked. To be honest, this Rocky guy sounded pretty boring.

Dad's fists fell to his sides. "No, he doesn't blow anything up. Well, not in this movie, at least."

I tried not to look too disappointed. I forced a big grin and imagined a giant rock man exploding. That was better.

"Oh, never mind," Dad said. "Let's get going!"

Dad moved his little dance-trot forward and spun around to face me.

"C'mon, son!" He clapped like Fart Lady and threw his hands in the air. "Pick up those feet!"

I jogged forward toward Dad. Every bit of me jiggled. Every. Single. Last. Bit. My belly bounced up and down. My upper arms flapped. My cheeks wobbled. Even my tongue felt loose. Like I'd been hastily put together with an old bottle of glue. The kind that'd been sitting in a desk drawer for ten years and was all crusty around the orange cap. Barf.

"Let's go! You can do it, Far!" Dad continued jogging backward, not even breaking a sweat. He was still doing that ridiculous *Rocky*-Philadelphia dance thingy, swatting at some invisible opponent standing on the sidewalk between us. "One foot in front of the other, son. One foot in front of the other!"

He spun around and tagged mailboxes and road signs as we pressed forward.

I did my best not to cause an earthquake.

I panted.

I sweated.

I shook and ached.

But I had to keep going. New Farley was in there somewhere, under all those layers.

One foot . . .

Oh, who was I kidding?

I had to stop. I bent over and rested my hands on my knees, gasping for air. I could almost see the puffs of steam coming off my overheating head. My body still quivered, even though technically I'd stopped moving. Every muscle twitched. Sweat burned my eyes.

"Dad?" My voice was little more than a sputter, like a car that's about to run out of gas.

"Dad?" I said again. He was about twenty feet ahead, boxing a stop sign post. I wasn't sure who was winning. Probably Dad. That's just how it is to be David Turner. A winner. *Take that, signpost!* Birds sang in glory around his head. A beam of sunlight shone through the clouds and illuminated his golden skin.

"Oh, hey, Far!" He did a couple of jumping jacks and swung his hands to his toes. "What's up?"

I shrugged.

Dad jogged back over. "You're not ready to stop yet, are you?"

I nodded. This was the one thing I was good at: being a disappointment to Dad.

"Okay, well, let's just take a quick breather." He pulled a bottle of water from the black leather pack around his waist. "Have a drink," he said. "It'll make you feel better."

I took a big swig of cold water while Dad marched in place.

"Thanks, Dad."

"Sure." He swung his head around and cracked his neck. "Ready to move on? Pow-pow! KO!" *Dance-shuffle-punch*.

Was he nuts?

Okay, stupid question.

I shook my head. "Not exactly," I puffed out.

Dad stretched his arms in the air and looked down the sidewalk toward our house. I turned around and looked too.

We'd gone precisely one block.

Pathetic.

That sinking feeling returned to the pit of my stomach.

"Hey, no worries, Far," Dad said, slapping my back. "We'll make it farther next time. Practice. Practice. Practice. Just like playing ball."

Right. My fears exactly.

"Gotta train those muscles," Dad said, adding a few jumping jacks to his routine. "Be running marathons before you know it."

Marathons? Dad had really lost it. Those things must be at least ten blocks.

"How 'bout we just walk a couple minutes?" he said. "Too soon to quit!"

I looked at Dad's relaxed, sweat-free face. He must really wonder how he got me as a kid. "Yeah, okay, Dad," I said. My shoulders drooped. It was the same old thing again. At some point you'd think Dad would just give up and see if he could exchange me for Burt or something.

We started walking, and Dad resumed his jabbering.

"You know, Far," he said, stretching his long arms above his head. "Back when I was a kid, we didn't have buses. Nope! We walked to school every day and . . ."

Blah, blah, blah. I knew. Uphill. Both ways. In a blizzard. Under threat of tsunami. And hurricane-force winds. While barefoot, right? Oh, and carrying seven thousand pounds of library books, homework assignments, and crucial supplies for the entire village, of course.

Okay. Got it.

"You see?" Dad said.

I just nodded as we reached the stop sign. Then I turned around and walked as slow as a turtle back home, bracing myself to see what Tomy had been up to in my brief absence.

10

"FENG SHOE?" I LOOKED AROUND MY ROOM AND rubbed my sore thighs. (Amazing how running all of two yards could turn my still nonexistent muscles into a quivering mess.)

"No. Feng shui," Tomy said proudly. He had taken a pair of my underpants and stretched them between my desk lamp and pencil holder, creating a little hammock for himself, where he swung serenely back and forth. "It means creating harmony between oneself and the environment. Becoming one with the wave!"

"Is that why my bed is in the middle of the room and my dresser is in the closet? And what about those?" I pointed at a half dozen rolled-up socks that had been arranged in a precise row along my windowsill.

"Meditation cushions!" Tomy exclaimed. "Sorry,

dude—but you'll just have to pretend they are facing the sunrise over the ocean."

There was a light rap on the door. Before I could answer, it pushed open. Mom stood on the other side.

"Oh," she said. "You've . . . redecorated?" Her eyes lingered for a moment on the bed, my hamper (which had been flipped over and the dirty clothes folded neatly on top), the socks, the underpants hammock with Tomy hidden inside, and then quickly back at me. "It's . . . interesting." She gave me a quick don't-worry-I-still-love-you-even-if-you're-clearly-losing-it Mom smile.

"Um, yeah," I said. "Trying some Kung Pow."

Mom's eyebrows bunched together in confusion briefly. Then she flashed that smile again. "That's . . . very nice," she muttered.

I could feel the heat creeping across my cheeks. "Okay," I said. "Did you want something? I was just going to rest a little. All that running." I flashed a smile back at her.

"Oh, yes!" Mom said. "Right! I just came to tell you, Burt's on the phone."

"Oh, thanks," I said. "I'll be right down."

Mom walked out of my room and headed downstairs. I followed slowly, muscles aching and knees creaking and popping the whole way.

Now, you may be wondering why I had to go *down-stairs* to answer the phone. The answer is simple: because we only have one phone, and it's hooked to a wall in the kitchen. And if that's not weird enough, it's one of those phones with a curly white cord that attaches the receiver to the base, like you see in old movies and museums and on the Boomerang channel. Otherwise known as a real phone, according to Mom.

I don't know if Mom's sentimental or just cheap, but we must be the only people on earth who don't own a cordless phone. Even Grandma and Grandpa Turner have one, and they're both, like, a hundred years old. I guess to Mom's credit, at least she finally ditched her flip phone and got a smartphone last year, even if she won't get me one. But I think she only got that because she found out she could play Tetris on it.

I stopped next to the counter, and Mom handed me the white receiver. About twenty years of her orange makeup was smudged in the ear holes. Ick. I held the phone a half inch from my own ear.

"Yo, Squirt," I said.

"About time, Fart."

"Sorry. Just got home from a run," I said.

"A what?" Burt said. "Did you say run? Because it sure sounded like you said *run*. Since when do you run?"

"Never mind, Squirt," I said. "What's up?"

"Right! So, I had an idea."

"What kind of idea?" I asked. As long as it didn't involve moving, I was cool. I waited for Burt's answer and twirled that white cord around my fingers. That's the one thing it's good for—fidgeting.

"We should form a band! You, me, and Josh."

"Huh?" I said. "Why would we do that? We don't even know how to play any instruments."

"Who cares," Burt replied. "It's not like those guys in Five Seconds to Liftoff do either. It would be cool."

"Huh," I said, staring at the cord around my finger. How many times could I loop it?

"Besides," Burt added. "Everyone loves bands!"

"Wait," I said with a pause. "What do you mean *everyone*?" I've known Burt for most of my life now. And I know when Burt is up to something. Which, to be honest, is most of the time.

"Oh," he said nonchalantly (Big Word of the Week #43, which means "coolly unconcerned." Or, in Burt's case, trying to act like he's not plotting anything). "Just . . . people."

"Any people in particular?" I asked, getting suspicious.

"I don't know," Burt said. "Just people."

I dropped the phone cord. Didn't even make it to

fourteen loops. Darn. "I don't suppose you mean girl people," I said.

Burt was silent.

I got even more suspicious. Was this about Addison Jenkins's survey? Or, even worse . . . What if I wasn't the only one who was trying to step up his game because Anna was back in town? Worse still—what if they'd already run into each other and he didn't tell me because it was love at first sight and they were already Snapchatting puppies? Poor Addison Jenkins. Poor *me*!

"Aww, c'mon, Fart!" Burt said. "I've got it all figured out. Josh has that drum set, and you've got that electric guitar thing you got a couple years ago for your birthday. That's all we need!"

"Seriously? That's not a real guitar, though," I said. "It's, like, the size of a violin! I got it when I was seven!"

"Yeah, but it makes music! That's all that matters. Anyway, all we need to do is look cool. And we're golden."

Easy for Burt to say. He wasn't going to be holding a violin-sized toy guitar in this imaginary band of his. Plus, he looks cool falling in ditches on field trips.

"What are you going to play, then?" I asked. "The recorder?"

"What?" Burt laughed. "I don't know how to play anything. So I just figured I'd be the lead singer."

Oh, great. Even better. Nobody remembers anyone's name in a band—except for the lead singer's. That's a documented fact. It's been scientifically proven at least a thousand times on the Internet and in those really ridiculous papers Mom pretends not to read at the supermarket checkout stand.

"So?" he asked. "Are you in? It'll be awesome. We'll rock!"

I didn't say anything.

"C'mon, man," Burt said. "I don't want to do it without you!"

Hold up. *Without me?*

"Sure. Okay." I sighed. "I'm in."

"Good! Come over today after lunch. I gotta go. I'm gonna call Josh."

"Okay, bye."

"Bye. Oh yeah, and don't forget your guitar!"

I dug the guitar out of my old toy box, stuck Tomy in my hood for safekeeping, went into the office, and asked Mom for a ride to Burt's.

"Burt's?" she said, glancing up from her computer. "Sure. That's perfect!"

"Perfect?" Mom never gets this excited about driving me anywhere. Most of the time I'm interrupting a critical mission, like working or restocking our pantry with enough canned food to survive a zombie apocalypse.

I followed Mom into the kitchen. She grabbed a tray of plastic-wrapped cookies from the counter and shoved them in my hands. I recoiled. Was this some sort of test?

"I don't want these," I said, even though my mouth was watering.

"Oh, they're not for you, honey," Mom said. "They're for the Murphys."

"Excuse me?" My heart started pounding a hundred thousand beats per second.

"I know," Mom said. "I feel terrible. They've been here nearly a week already and I haven't stopped by to welcome them back. You remember the Murphys, right? You and their littlest used to be buddies way back in the day. It'll be nice to see them again!" She grabbed the car keys and headed toward the garage. "Come on. Let's go!"

I walked behind her carrying the cookies, leaving a trail of nervous sweat in my wake, and climbed into my designated seat in the minivan. My nerves turned to sheer terror as Mom drove out of the garage and turned down Gentle Way, singing along to the radio.

I gotta feeling—ooh, ooh!—that tonight's gonna be a good night!

I would argue otherwise.

I slid down in my seat and stared at the tray, trying to come up with a way out of this visit. What if I just gobbled up all these cookies so there was nothing to drop off? No. Bad idea. Tomy might revoke one of my scrolls for that. Alternate plan: Mom could drop me off at Burt's first.

Mom rolled to a stop—in front of the Murphys'—and put the car in park.

Crud.

I leaned forward to hand her the cookies. It was okay; she could do it. "Here you go. . . ."

Her phone rang.

There was a heavy sigh from the driver's seat. "I'm sorry, Farley," she said. "I have to get this. It's a client. Could you run those cookies in? Tell Mrs. Murphy I'll call her soon."

Noooooooo!

I searched for a place to hide. Mom spun around and gave me that what-are-you-waiting-for look she likes to deploy when I'm being too slow putting on my shoes to catch the school bus in the morning. She waved her hand at me and pointed toward the Murphy house, then tapped her phone screen.

"Why, yes, hello, Mr. McCormick!" she said. "No, no. Don't worry. I do still think Helvetica perfectly conveys the whimsy of your accounting firm! Sure, but . . ."

I trudged from the car and began the long, treacherous slog up the walkway, practicing what I'd say in my mind.

Hello, Anna. Welcome back! Maybe you remember me? Farley from first grade? Yes, I realize I haven't changed one bit. But I stopped eating paste, so I have that going for me, right?

Yuck. No. Wait. I had a better idea!

Welcome, new neighbors! I'm . . . Melville. Just wanted to drop these cookies off. Sorry to say, you won't be seeing me again because I'm moving tomorrow. Oh, I look familiar? You must be thinking of that kid Farley. Yeah, I wish. I'll probably never be that buff. Nice to meet you, though—sorry it'll be the last time!

Yeah, that was it. *Melville.* Tomy popped his head over my shoulder and began sniffing the air. "What is that delicious aroma? Like coconut oil and chocolate!"

I shoved him back into my hood, sucked in a breath, and rang the doorbell.

Footsteps echoed across the hardwood inside.

Clack, clack, clack . . .

I stood up straight. Melville, I'm *Melville*. . . .

The door flung open.

"Farley!"

I nearly jumped out of my shoes.

"It's so great to see you again!" Mrs. Murphy said. "Look at you, all grown up now, but I'd recognize you anywhere!"

Of course she would. Yay, me.

Mrs. Murphy flung her arms around me and gave me a big hug, nearly knocking the cookies from my hands.

"Oh, sorry!" she said, releasing me with a little shoulder pat.

"It's okay. These are for you." I held out the tray. All the cookies had slid sideways and were jumbled underneath the plastic wrap. "My mom wanted to come up, but she's stuck on a client call." I looked back at the minivan. Mom waved, rolled her eyes, and pointed at the phone. Mrs. Murphy waved back and smiled.

"Tell your mom thanks," she said.

I nodded and glanced past Mrs. Murphy, stomach in knots. There were boxes and piles of packing paper everywhere, furniture shoved against walls . . .

"Anna!" Mrs. Murphy shouted.

Ack! Was it too late to change my name to Melville? How fast could I run back to the minivan?

A red-haired head poked around the corner from the kitchen.

"Uh, Mom . . . , " came the deep voice of one of Anna's twin brothers. "She's not here, remember?"

Mrs. Murphy tapped her own forehead. "Of course," she said. "Sorry, Farley. I got so excited I forgot Anna left this morning for basketball camp. But I'll make sure she gives you a shout when she gets back. She's going to be so happy to hear you stopped by!"

11

I GRABBED MY GUITAR FROM THE MINIVAN AND jogged across the street to Burt's, Tomy bouncing in my hood, my heart pounding. I wasn't really sure how many more close calls like this I could handle. How was I supposed to hide from Anna all summer with her living right across the street from my best friend?

I went upstairs to Burt's room, where Josh and Burt were waiting for me to jam. Although truth be told, the first half hour of band practice didn't involve much jamming at all. That's because we were totally stumped on the most important thing—a name. We ruled out the Gladiators, Fish Breath, and Rock Rangers. Turns out those were already taken. We looked them up online. (And trust me, you don't want to see Fish

Breath. They pretty much look like you might expect, only grosser and with more hair than scales.)

"I vote for the Burt-Tones," Burt said from his top bunk, where he was noodling band names over the latest *Planet of Doom* comic. A giant piece of new, thick wood had been nailed beneath the mattress to hold it in place. Needless to say, I was sticking with the safety of the floor.

"The Burt-Tones?" Josh said. "That sounds like something my great-grandpa would listen to!"

"Yeah? Well, the band was my idea and I'm the lead singer," Burt answered. "So I should get to name it." He loudly flipped the pages. "After myself."

"So?" said Josh. "We're still not calling it something as stupid as the Burt-Tones!"

"Well," I said. "I vote for the Farley Project, then."

"That's even stupider!" Burt said. "I still think the Burt-Tones is good."

The little voice in my hood piped up. "Remember, you can't have music without harmony! No waves without the moon!" Yeah, I'd seen Tomy's moon already. Twice. I could definitely live without it.

"Keep it down!" I hissed back.

"Keep it down?" Burt said. "What's up with that?"

"Sorry, I wasn't talking to—"

"Actually," Josh said, "I kind of like that. It's ironic,

right? 'Cause we'll be making music. Keep it down. KID for short!"

Burt shook his head. "Sounds too much like what my mom says when she gives me cough medicine." He stuck out his tongue and gagged.

Josh tapped his drumsticks on the edge of Burt's bed and pointed one up in the air. "Well, I know, then! How about Josh and the Squirt Farts?" He cracked up.

"Ha-ha," said Burt.

"Ha-ha-ha," I added.

"The Squirt Farts!" Josh snorted and fell over on Darren's bunk, clutching his sticks to his belly. He began hyperventilating and making pig noises. For a minute I thought we might have to call 911. It looked like he'd stopped breathing.

This was getting ridiculous.

Burt kept thumbing through his *Dr. Fantastic* and muttered "Burt-Tones" for the hundred thousandth time. I heard the basketball bouncing and peeked outside through the curtains even though I knew Anna wouldn't be out there. It was just her twin brothers, Leo and Al. I had a vague, and not terribly pleasant, memory of those two constantly pranking us when we were little. (Just in case you were curious, sponge cake—made from an actual sponge—is *not* particularly tasty, even if it is smothered in strawberry frosting.)

"Hold up!" I said, looking at the glossy pages on Burt's lap. "How about the Fantastics?"

Burt's eyebrows arched. "Hmmm. The Fantastics? Yeah," he said, nodding. "That's not bad. If it can't be the Burt-Tones, I mean."

"You can't name a band after a comic book." Josh groaned.

"Why not?" Burt asked.

"We'll never have any fans! Girls don't like comic books!" Josh said. "Don't you two know anything?"

"Oh, like you're such an expert," Burt said. "That whole thing with Kaitlyn Duggan really proves that."

Josh totally had a thing for this girl Kaitlyn in our class last year. So, his big idea was to follow her around and try to impress her by making fart noises with his armpits. It worked about as well as you might expect. Now Kaitlyn—and pretty much half of our class, for that matter—go the other way whenever they see Josh coming, especially if he's scratching his pits.

Josh swung a drumstick in the direction of Burt's head.

Burt ducked and sang, "Oh, Kaaaaaiiiitlyyyyyyyyn," and started making kissing noises.

"Shut up," Josh said. "I still know more than you two idiots."

"Whatever," Burt said, slapping his comic shut. "We're going with the Fantastics. You're outvoted."

"Huh," said Josh. "We'll always be Josh and the Squirt Farts as far as I'm concerned." He stuck his right hand under his left armpit and started producing his infamous squeaky fart noises while dancing around the room singing "squirt farts, squirt farts!"

Burt and I ignored him.

"Okay," said Burt. "Now that we have a name, we need to practice a song. What do you guys know how to play?"

"Well . . ." I pulled out my guitar. "This thing only has seven songs programmed into it. So it's gonna have to be one of those. And they're all, like, a thousand years old."

Josh stared at the toy instrument in my hand a moment, then snorted. "Dude! Who are we playing for? The Happy Garden Preschool?"

He and Burt both laughed. The tips of my ears burned. "It's just for practice," I mumbled. "Until I save up enough for a real one."

"Don't worry," Burt said. "Once the Fantastics are rich and famous, you can definitely afford a real guitar. Or at least a *Barney & Friends* subwoofer to match!"

Josh snorted. Burt smoothed out his T-shirt. "And

I'm gonna get a studded leather jacket and maybe some boots with big buckles. . . ." He kicked his leg in the air. Josh rolled his eyes.

"So, what does that thing play?" he said, pointing a drumstick in my direction. "And I'm *not* jamming to 'Twinkle, Twinkle, Little Star'!"

"I dunno," I said. "The only one I've ever heard of is 'Wild Thing.' I saw it once on that car commercial for Harris Motors."

"'Wild Thing' it is," Burt said. "Fire it up!"

I cranked the black knob on my toy guitar to the last click and set it to song six. The frets started flashing red. I put my left hand over the blinking lights and strummed with my right. Well, fake strummed. There are strings and everything to make it look like a real guitar, but they don't actually make any sound. They're just for show. The "music" comes out of a small speaker on the back.

Bum-bum-bum . . . bum-bum-be-bum, the guitar hummed.

"Cool!" Burt yelled.

Josh tapped his drumsticks to the beat on Burt's desk. The drums were back at Josh's house because they're too hard to pack and carry upstairs to Burt's room.

"So, what are the words?" Burt asked.

"I dunno," I said. "I think it's just 'Wild Thing' over and over. We can look 'em up later."

"Cool," Burt said. "I can do that."

He started dancing around the room, singing into his Coke bottle. *Wild thing! Yeah, yeah, yeah, wild thing.* " He kicked his leg up in the air and pumped the bottle about fifty times over his head. That thing was gonna explode when Burt opened it up for a drink later. I made a mental note to stand back.

Josh tapped the sticks harder and added a little butt shake to his routine. Burt kept sing-yelling, "*Wild thing! Yeah, yeah, yeah!*"

I threw a little extra muscle into the fake guitar strumming, and we all sang along.

"*Wild Thing! Yeah, yeah, yeah, yeah!*"

Burt's pet hamster, Rufus, started going nuts in his cage, running in circles and sending wood chips flying in every direction. Burt's little sister, Greta, stopped and stared at us from the door before hightailing it off with her tiny hands clapped over her ears and her mouth frozen in a silent scream. Darren was nowhere in sight. He'd pretty much been steering clear of me and Burt since the fateful collapsing-bunk incident. I could even feel Tomy dancing in my hood. It tickled.

Wild Thing! Yeah, yeah, yeah, yeah!

* * *

When I got home, I clicked on the next scroll:

Step Four: Step Out of Your Comfort Zone!
Remember, you are the driving force
behind your own change. Congratulate
yourself! Then find at least one way to do
something that would have made the old you
uncomfortable. Each time you do so, you move
one step closer to the new you. This is hard! So
don't forget to pat yourself on the back!

Well, as far as I could tell, this should be the easiest step of all—this entire experiment was 100 percent outside of my comfort zone, not to mention I'd just been playing a *toy guitar* in a band.

So why wasn't that scroll disappearing in a poof of glitter?

I tried patting myself on the back. Several times.

Nope?

Okay, maybe another run with Dad would do the trick.

12

THE NEXT MORNING DAD AND I STOOD AT THE end of our driveway again in our running gear: Dad in his sleek spandex suit with matching headband and me in his old stretchy shorts and my *Dr. Fantastic* shirt. I left Tomy with precise orders not to go out, be seen, or touch *any* of my stuff.

"Okay, Far," Dad said. "Today we're going to make it all the way to the second stop sign." He pointed to the far end of the road. I had to squint to see it. It was like a mirage in the desert, shimmering there on an endless stretch of black asphalt.

"Three blocks, Dad? Seriously?"

"Yep. And back, too. And by the end of the summer, we'll get all the way to Burt's!"

"Burt's? That's gotta be a mile!"

"Sure is, Far," Dad said. "And a mile back, too!"

Old Farley groaned inside. New Farley said, "Great, Dad." *Think marathon, Farley. Marathon.*

"Okay, here we go! First let's stretch." Dad put his arms out wide. "Do what I do, Far."

He turned his long, thin body like a licorice stick and touched his left foot with his right hand. Then he touched his right foot effortlessly with his left hand. He did this ten times in perfect windmill form.

I leaned forward as far as I could and swatted at the stale, hot air around my knees.

Dad put his hands on his hips and twisted side to side.

I did the same, each turn folding Dr. Fantastic's head in half.

Dad reached down and grabbed his right knee and pulled it tight to his chest. Left knee, repeat.

I stretched for my knee and kicked my foot out a little. All I could see was the tip of my scuffed sneakers past all those layers of Farley.

"Okay, Far!" he said, capping off his stretches with a round of jumping jacks. "Let's move it!" He clapped. And we were off.

It was a pleasant, sunny day in the "idyllic, family-friendly" neighborhood of Gentle Cove (even if there is no cove anywhere to be found—in fact, the closest body of water is Josh's pool, I think). Mom says this whole place was just a big cornfield when she was little. Now it's a hundred identical houses with brick on the fronts and matching mailboxes and rows of tidy green shrubs lining the curb. I used to wish all the carefully spaced storm drains around the neighborhood were actually portals to other places and if you climbed in you'd wind up in another identical neighborhood. Say, in Cleveland or somewhere cool-sounding like that.

But no, all that happens is you get stuck.

Dad and I ran, while all around us Saturday morning happened—lawn mowers rattled, weed whackers buzzed, little kids on tricycles clattered along driveways, yelling and laughing. Freshly cut grass stuck to the bottom of my rapidly slowing sneakers. *I'm . . . never . . . gonna . . . make . . . it.*

Meanwhile, Dad trotted ahead and waved to the neighbors like he was on a parade route.

"Howdy, Mr. Burke!" he said, knees pumping double time. "Hello, Mrs. Dryer!" His hand shot in the air and his fingers wiggled.

I kept my focus straight ahead. I didn't particularly want to see the expression on everyone's faces as I trudged past. I was well aware of how ridiculous I looked. A big, bouncing ball of Farley lunging down the street, shaking apples off trees and scaring squirrels from the bushes.

"Almost there, Far!" Dad hollered back. "You know, Far, the key to muscle endurance is the repetition of motion and continued conditioning of the lateral . . ."

"Uh-huh." I panted. I couldn't hear a word he was saying anymore as he disappeared up the street, his long pointer finger still up in the air. My body began to droop. I should have been used to this feeling. After all, this was my usual view of Dad—from a distance, left in the dust. Still, I wished that for once he'd just *stop*. Turn around and notice I wasn't right behind him and give me a chance to actually catch up.

Dad tagged the signpost, did a couple of jumping jacks, then began the round-trip home.

"Hello, Mrs. Dryer!" He waved.

"Howdy, Mr. Burke!" He dance-punched.

"Don't give up now, Far!" he said, passing me with a wide grin pressed across his cheeks.

Rattle went the lawn mowers. *Buzz* went the weed whackers. *Yippee, woo!* went the little kids.

I went slower . . .

And slower . . .

And slower.

Dad was already back on the front steps doing his super stretches when I reached the post. *Tag. Pant. Pant. Turn around. Squint for home. Start running again.*

I morphed into a rock. No, not a rock—a zombie. A big, dead zombie dragging my big dead legs across the pavement. My big dead arms dangled in the air. My big dead tongue flopped from my big dead mouth. Little kids abandoned their tricycles, screamed, and ran to the safe arms of their mommies. Vultures circled overhead. The sky grew dark and ominous. Thunder crashed. Old ladies made the sign of the cross over their chests and wept into scrunched-up white handkerchiefs.

But I made it. Finally. Just before the entire world exploded and collapsed on itself, like in *Dr. Fantastic* episode 461.

"Practice! Practice! Practice!" Dad said with a corresponding *thud* on my back. "Just like playing ball!"

Poor, rusted zombie-Farley shattered into a thousand pieces all over the neatly swept brick front steps.

This was hopeless.

13

FAST-FORWARD TWO WEEKS AND TWELVE MORE runs with Dad, ugh—and nothing had changed. I didn't feel any different. Just *sore*. Scroll four: *Step Out of Your Comfort Zone* remained in its unfurled position on my computer screen. Apparently, my comfort zone knew no bounds. At least I hadn't bumped into Anna. I was sure she had to be back from basketball camp at this point, but she never seemed to be outside when I went to Burt's, so that was a relief.

I hobbled into my seat at our kitchen table, Tomy in my hood meditating on a ball of rolled-up socks. Every time he exhaled, it felt like a tiny spider running across the back of my neck. I shuddered and stared at my breakfast: a rice cake smudged with low-fat peanut butter. Two shriveled-up prunes perched alongside looked back at me like a pair of rotten eyeballs.

Gross.

I picked up the rice cake and took a bite. *Phwlat!* It tasted like a Styrofoam cup. And I knew that for a fact. Burt had dared me to eat a piece of one in the fourth grade.

I nibbled the slimy prune. Double gross. Who knew there was something worse than boiled food? I had no idea how long I could keep this up.

"Is everything okay, Farley?" Mom asked. "Prunes were on your list, right?"

"Yeah, they're great, Mom," New Farley said. Old Farley gagged.

Mom and Dad poured syrup on their fluffy toaster waffles. I could almost taste their buttery goodness. . . .

Word of the day: famished. As in, Farley was so famished he had nightmares about The Online Master's floating head gobbling up the Twinkies next to his bed like Pac-Man. *Famished.*

"So," Dad said. "I think I'll head to the gym for a few this morning." He tapped his already flat stomach.

"Sounds nice," Mom said.

"Remember!" a voice piped up from somewhere behind

my left ear. "You can only conquer the wave by riding it!"

I jolted, and my chair thumped. "How many times do I have to tell you to be quiet!" I said over my shoulder.

"Farley!" Dad said sternly. "Did you just tell your mother to be quiet?"

"Ah, no. No!" I said, thinking fast. "I just said it would be . . . *quite* . . . uh . . . quite nice to go to the gym with you today!" I swallowed a clump of dry rice cake and forced a smile.

Dad's left eyebrow poked up. "You want to come to the gym?"

Okay, I was definitely out of my comfort zone here. I avoid gyms like I do art projects.

"Yeah. There must be something, uh, fun I could do there. Dead lifts, maybe?"

Dad shook his head. "Don't think you're quite ready for that yet. We'll move on to weight training when you're a little older."

Humph. Guess that didn't involve zombies . . . Too bad.

"But!" Dad said. "There's a climbing wall downstairs. That looks like fun."

Mom dropped her fork. It rattled in protest on the table. "Oh, honey, do you think that's a good idea?"

"Why not?" Dad asked.

"Well." Mom paused. "Isn't it a little . . . ?" She glanced at Dad without looking at me. "Isn't a climbing wall a little *dangerous*?" She whispered "dangerous" in her super-secret Mom voice. The one she thinks I can't hear, even if I'm sitting right next to her. I was actually rather surprised she didn't try spelling it.

"It's perfectly safe, honey," Dad said in his booming lawyer voice. "He's not a baby."

"Can I? Can I go with Dad?"

Mom puzzled over the syrup container for a minute. Like maybe it was a Magic 8-Ball and there was a little triangle answer in there getting ready to float up to the top.

"Well, can I?" If I didn't get myself past step four, I'd be graduating from college with Tomy hidden under my cap. Also, patience isn't exactly my best virtue.

Mom's mouth twisted sideways. She spun the waffle on her plate. She inspected her pink fingernails and clucked her tongue.

"Sure, Farley. If your dad thinks it's okay, I think it's great. Maybe I'll go to the library."

"Excellent!" Dad said. "Far, finish your breakfast and we'll get out of here!"

I held my nose and quickly inserted the remaining rice cake and prunes down the slot. *Glug. Glug. Gag!*

"Hey, Mom?" I said with a cough.

"Yeah, Far?"

"Would you mind picking me up a book while you're at the library?"

This brightened Mom's face. "Why, yes! I'd love to. Do you have anything in mind?"

"Yes, actually," I said, pushing a stuck piece of prune off my back tooth with my tongue. "*War and Peace.*"

This time it was Dad's fork that rattled to the table. "*War and Peace*, Far?"

"Yeah. Is there something wrong with that?" My belly got a strange squiggly feeling, and I hoped this wasn't about to go the way of the "derriere" fiasco.

"Um, no," Dad said. "It's just a little . . . ambitious."

"Well, it's for school," I lied, breathing a sigh of relief.

"They're assigning Tolstoy now as seventh-grade summer reading?"

I shrugged. "Extra credit?"

Dad's mouth opened to speak, but Mom shot him a funny look and shook her head. He bit a piece of waffle instead. What was that all about?

"I'd be happy to get you anything you'd like," she said. *Go, Farley!*

Take that, tiny surfer dude in my hoodie!

* * *

I felt like a giant ham tied up in string—the kind Mom buys every Easter and serves with little candied pineapple slices and a side of yams smothered in toasty marshmallows. Mmmm . . . marshmallows. Crispy on the outside, melty in the middle, soft and sweet and . . . *Get a grip, Farley! Must. Stop. Thinking. About. Food.* I adjusted the big canvas thing strapped under my butt and tugged at the thick straps wrapped around my body. A long, heavy rope ran from a hook on my back to a pulley on the ceiling. A big guy named Kev held the other end. Any minute now I'd be dangling from the wall, the ceiling, or both.

Now that I thought about it, maybe I wasn't exactly a ham. I was more like a piñata. But one full of rice cake and prunes instead of candy.

And maybe, for once in my life, I just wanted be a person—not a jumble of food and fart jokes. Was that too much to ask?

"Okay, Farley!" Kev yelled from behind my piñata-strung self. Kev had really thick arm muscles sticking out from his electric-blue Middleford Health Club tank top, which was good since Kev and that rope were all that stood between Farley and the floor. "Okay. Put your right foot on that blue hold right there. Excellent! Now reach up for the yellow holds and pull yourself up."

Easy for Kev to say.

I stretched my right arm as far as it would go and grabbed for the fake rock thingy poking out from the wall. Much to my surprise, I got it. My left hand arched toward the other one. Got that, too! I lifted my left leg off the ground and plunked it on another piece of plastic rock. The rope on my back snapped tight.

Holy moly, I was on the wall!

I am Spider-Man!

Forget Batman. New Farley climbs walls like Spider-Man!

Go, Farley!

Okay, so I was only one inch off the ground. But I wasn't falling off, was I?

I was *Spider-Man*! Huzzah!

"Great job," Kev said. "Now pull yourself up on your left foot and reach to the next level of holds."

I squished my left cheek on the hard plastic wall and shimmied upward, suddenly forgetting how ridiculous I probably looked.

"Keep going! You can do it, Farley!"

I grabbed another hold.

I lifted another foot. And another. And another. I kept going until the drips of sweat in my eyes made the wall all fuzzy-looking. I grabbed a last hold. Way. Up. High.

I did it!

"Awesome!" Kev yelled from the floor below. He was so far away, he looked like a little ant down there. Okay, maybe not exactly, but I was still at the top. Who cared if it was only ten feet up and I was just on the training wall?

"Now," Kev said, "the best part. When you're ready, kick off the wall and bounce down. I'll have your rope. Trust me, okay?"

I gulped. Farley and gravity are not good friends.

"Trust me," Kev said again. "I've been doing this forever. You're gonna love it! Just tell me when you're ready."

I took a deep breath and looked to the left. On the other side of the glass wall that separates the climbing room from the rest of the gym, I spotted Dad. Watching. And he was smiling. Not that pretending-to-be-happy smile from my Little League days when I'd struck out for the gazillionth time and had to trudge back to the dugout, my brand-new, never dented Louisville Slugger bat dragging in the dirt behind me. No, this time it was a real way-to-go smile. I smiled back and waved.

"Ready!" I yelled, and I kicked my feet off the wall. "Cannnn-onnnnn-ballllllll!"

Then the most amazing thing ever happened.

I was flying!

Down . . .

Down . . .

Down . . .

For a few incredible seconds, gravity lost hold of Farley and I was as free and light as a bird.

It was just as good—maybe even better—than floating in Josh's pool.

There was no stopping New Farley now! I'd completely blasted myself out of my comfort zone.

But later, when I got back to my room, that darn blinking fourth scroll was still there.

And *War and Peace* was sitting on my desk.

14

SPOILER ALERT: *WAR AND PEACE* IS NOT A BOOK.

It's got words in it and everything. But it's not a book. It's more like an asteroid or a piece of satellite that crashed to earth. There's probably a giant smoking crater wherever it landed, surrounded by a bunch of guys from Area 51 who are trying to determine if it's here to kill all of mankind. (It is.)

I lifted the monstrosity with two hands and heaved it onto my bed. Tomy bounced about a foot in the air and landed on my pillow.

"Sorry, dude," I said.

He smoothed his beach-dress and sat. The book sank deep in the covers and disappeared. Man, maybe I could just exercise with that thing instead of running with Dad every day. I glanced at the computer, where scroll four was still open and brightly lit. Ugh. How big was this comfort zone of mine anyway?

Tomy nodded at my book.

"Every story begins at the first page. . . ."

Right. I knew that. And there was no way I was skipping to the ending. I'd learned my lesson. I didn't need to manifest a war into my bedroom. Although . . .

Nah, that would just get me in more trouble.

I sat down and opened the heavy cover. Crud. No pictures, either. I had better start reading if I expected to finish sometime this century.

Okay, first paragraph. We've got a prince. We've got infamies and horrors. That sounded promising. But wait. We've got someone with the "grippe." The what?

I'd better read that again.

I was still lost.

Where were the battles? Where was the horror?

There was an awful lot of talking going on here.

Eyelids getting heavy . . .

Must persevere. Grippe, grippe, grippe. Party invitations. Scarlet-liveried footmen.

Eyelids drooping . . .

Princes speaking languidly.

Snore.

* * *

"Fart!" It was Burt, and he was all wound up about something, breathing heavy into the phone.

"Hey, Squirt," I said, rubbing the pillow creases from my cheek. "What's up?"

"Fart, you've got to get over here. Now!" He was talking almost too fast to understand, like a video playing in forward scan.

"Huh, why?" I walked around the corner and sat on the steps to the family room. That silly twisted phone cord pulled tight on the wall behind me. Most likely it was adding another scuff mark to the white paint, which is why I was not supposed to talk in here. Oh well. My feet were tired, especially after all that running and climbing. I yanked the cord a little harder and tried to get comfortable.

"My mom invited Anna over."

"Wait. Did you say *Anna*?" I gulped.

"Yes, Anna," he said. "My mom talked to her mom and invited her over. *Today!*" Burt's voice went all high and squeaky, like when we sucked all the helium out of his birthday balloons once. He paused to catch his breath.

"Okay, so what's the big deal?" I tried to sound casual, but I'm pretty sure my voice was squeaking even more than Burt's.

"Big deal?" Burt said. "Are you kidding me? She's, like,

not a little kid anymore. We don't know what she's into. What if she doesn't like *Dr. Fantastic*? Or video games?" He paused and sucked in a sharp breath. "*What if she brings her scissors?* DO YOU HAVE ANY IDEA HOW LONG IT TAKES MY HAIR TO GROW OUT?!"

"I'm sure it's not that bad. . . ."

"You don't know that," Burt said. "You've got to get over here!"

"Um, yeah. I'm not sure . . ."

I mean, New Farley wasn't ready. New Farley wasn't even close to ready. New Farley hadn't even made it four blocks or past the languid prince.

"Why did your mom invite her over without asking you first, anyway?" I said.

"Something about Anna's mom saying how she's been kinda bummed out since they got here, missing her friends back in Italy, and how she's been spending too much time alone," Burt said. "I don't know. Just meddling mom stuff!"

"Oh." I was suddenly hit by a memory, back when I first knew Anna in preschool. Our class was taking a field trip to the zoo, and all the other kids were arguing over who got to sit next to her on the bus. Well, except me. I was sitting alone feeling sorry for myself, since Burt had rolled in poison ivy over the weekend and was back home, covered in crusty pink lotion and trying not to scratch.

But then—for reasons I could never totally understand—Anna walked up the aisle and sat next to me and gave me half of her granola bar.

"Fart? Are you there?" Burt interrupted my stroll down memory lane.

"Yeah, I'm here. When's she coming over?"

"At two o'clock," Burt said. "Please? Can you come over at one? Please? I'm begging you! In the name of Dr. Fantastic and all that is holy and sacred!"

"All right, Burt. I'll come over," I said. "But one thing."

"What is it, Fart?"

"Don't call me Fart," I said. "Farley. Call me Farley."

"Oh, okay, Fart . . . ley. Farley. Okay, I promise to call you Farley."

"Okay, Burt. See you at one, then."

"Okay, bye."

I was about to say bye back when that twirly white cord popped out of the phone base and zinged me right in the center of the forehead. *Ouch!* That stung. I rubbed my noggin with my right hand. Man, I didn't even realize I was pulling it so hard.

Sorry, Mom.

* * *

"I have nothing to wear!" I pulled shirt after bunched-up shirt from my dresser and dumped them in a heap on the floor. "Too big. Too ugly. Too . . ." I held one up and sniffed. "Covered in ketchup. Yuck!"

This was hopeless. I mean, Old Farley never concerned himself with something as stupid as clothes. Everything in my wardrobe was just a variation of pants/shorts with an elastic waist and giant T-shirts. Oh, and a couple of dress shirts Mom stuffs me into for church and every Christmas for family pictures.

I yanked on my oversized T-shirt with the stretched-out collar. "I can't go over to Burt's house looking like . . . this!"

"Remember," Tomy said. "To master the wave, you must find your center!"

"Huh? I just need to find some pants!"

In a state of panic, I snagged the box of Twinkies off my nightstand and jammed my hand inside. One, two, three, four, five, six, seven. Maybe one wouldn't hurt. Just one. To take the edge off. *Nope!* I licked my lips and slapped the box back down.

I began to hyperventilate.

"There is nothing so gnarly that a calm, cleansing breath can't help," Tomy said. I glanced at him sitting on my mouse pad. He nodded, then placed his hand on his crossed knees, closed his eyes, and inhaled deeply.

"Feel the wave. Find your focus. Ahhhhhhh . . ."

I took a couple of shallow breaths and thought I might faint. "Sorry! Not working!"

I returned to my dresser, opened the middle drawer, threw a bunch of stuff onto the floor, and wiggled my hand all the way to the back. Eventually, my fingers reached one ball of crumpled-up fabric. I yanked it out.

Finally! A pair of not-too-disgusting khaki shorts.

I changed into those.

But the shirt? That was a lost cause. I tried one of my old fancy dress shirts hanging in the closet. Oh, help me. Long sleeves. Buttons didn't reach across the front anymore. Fantastic. I yanked it off and watched it land in a pile of blue pinstripes on the floor.

"Help!" I said.

"I have an idea!" Tomy said.

"Yeah?"

"Sometimes you just need to get away from it all. The soothing sound of the surf always helps me think. . . . Let's hit the beach!" He grabbed his surfboard.

"Nice try . . ." I squinted at him, but then I thought a minute. "Hold on! You might be onto something!"

"Rad! Let's go!"

"No. I mean you gave me another idea. Dad's 'resort wear'!"

I crept out my door and padded quietly down the carpeted hall to Dad's bedroom closet. There I found a whole row of button-down short-sleeved shirts covered in brightly colored palm trees and flowers that Dad brings on our family cruise every year. Fancy, but casual at the same time. In other words, *perfect*.

I slipped into a bright green one decorated with pineapples and coconuts. A little long, but I could tuck it in like Dad's always telling me to do anyway.

I dodged back out the door and collided head-on with Mom.

"Far!" she said. "What were you doing in our room?"

"Just borrowing a shirt."

"Why? Where are your shirts?"

"Uh," I said. "Dirty?" I tried the charm-smile that worked way back when I was four.

"Far," Mom said. "How many times do I have to tell you . . . ?"

"Yeah, yeah. I know. Put my hamper in the hall when I need clean clothes."

"That's right. Put your hamper in the hall. Is that too much to ask?"

"No, Mom. It isn't. And I will." I gave the charm-smile another shot.

"Well," she said, adjusting the collar on my shirt.

"You do look nice. A chip off the old block, I must say."

Or a block off the old chip was more like it.

"Thanks, Mom."

"So what are you all dressed up for anyway?"

"Uh, nothing." I looked past Mom at the big gold light that hangs over our stairs.

"I see. Nothing—" Mom said.

"Can I have a ride to Burt's?" I interrupted.

"Sure, hon," she said. "Just one thing first . . ."

"Okay."

Mom zipped into the bathroom and came out with her big-bristled hairbrush. "Hold still."

Normally, I run for the hills when Mom tries to detangle the knot of yarn that is my hair. But this time I stood real still and let her have at it. She combed it off to the side, then ran her fingers through the top and messed it up a little.

"Perfect," she said, leaning back and inspecting her work. "Just right for . . . for going to Burt's." She smiled and touched my cheek and looked at me in that silly way moms look at a kid like they're the greatest thing ever to set foot on Planet Earth.

"Thanks, Mom."

"No problem, Far. You're a good kid. Don't forget that. Okay?"

15

BURT AND I WERE IN HIS BASEMENT WHEN THE
doorbell rang. I heard Mrs. Miller open the front door,
then a bunch of *hi, how-are-yous*, and then she directed
Anna downstairs.

For a moment time froze.

I counted the steps as Anna descended. *Thirteen,
twelve, eleven . . .*

And I flashed back to when we all first met: in the
Fish Pond, when we were three years old. (FYI—the Fish
Pond is not actually a pond. It was the name of our preschool class, and we were the fish. Seriously, I don't know
who comes up with this stuff—I mean, they wouldn't
even let us play in the puddles during recess, let alone go
near a pond. Liability and all that. But whatever.)

So technically, I guess Burt officially met Anna first,

due to the whole Miller-Murphy alphabetical-seating-arrangement thing (and the fact that he accidentally squirted her in the face with his juice box during snack time, which is certainly one way to start a conversation).

But the truth is, I had spotted her on the very first day when she walked into the "pond" with a Cowgirl Jessie backpack hoisted over her shoulders. (Yes, I had a total *Toy Story* obsession back then. Spent most of the year dressed in a Buzz Lightyear costume and shouting "to infinity and beyond!" every time I went down the slide. Don't judge. You were three once too.)

Anyway, it turned out Anna also lived in the neighborhood, and so we all just kinda bonded in that little-kid way you do when proximity (and parents who like each other) puts you in the same orbit. Maybe not all that different from now, I suppose, with Mrs. Miller inviting Anna over . . .

The footsteps got closer. *Three, two, one . . .*

And just like that, Anna appeared in the doorway. I stood up straight. I'm not 100 percent sure what I expected—that she'd still have jelly beans hidden in her socks or would be missing her two front teeth? But I guess I wasn't totally 100 percent expecting her to be so . . . *Anna.*

Only better.

I mean, her eyes were still big and blue, and her hair was still golden-copper red. But it was in a high ponytail, not pigtails. And she'd grown taller and thinner and had sprouted a new row of sweet little freckles across her nose. Eight, to be exact. Not that I was counting or anything. She'd swapped out the Hello Kitty attire for a white T-shirt, jeans shorts, and tie-dyed high-top Converse sneakers. Her right wrist was covered in multicolored beaded bracelets.

"Hey, guys," she said with a little wave. The bracelets jangled. My heart inexplicably beat a little faster.

"Hey," Burt said. He crossed and uncrossed his arms, then leaned against the wall and stood up again. It was at this point that I really took notice of Burt's getup—a crisp button-down layered over his Minecraft T-shirt, hair neatly combed and parted down the middle. Clearly he'd actually showered, which went completely against Burt's summer motto of bathing only by sprinkler or pool.

"Hey," I said. "Welcome back." I sucked in my gut and felt an involuntary escape of air from the other end.

Ack!

I casually stepped in the direction of Burt. Maybe any smell would follow me there. Burt cleared his throat.

"Can I offer you a beverage?" he said, lowering his

voice and motioning toward the mini-fridge like a game-show host. "We have an excellent selection of soft drinks." I stared at him in disbelief. What was he doing? A half smile formed on Anna's face. She looked like she was trying not to laugh.

"No. I'm fine," she said. "Thanks for having me over. So, what do you guys want to do?"

Burt looked at me, panic creeping across his face. I made a little scissors motion across the front of my hair with my fingers. Burt's eyes widened.

"Up to you," he said, now looking at Anna. "You're the guest." This time his voice cracked.

"Great!" Anna said. "I was *really* hoping we could go out back and check for Hoppy. . . ."

Back in kindergarten, Anna found this toad she named Hoppy and decided to keep as a pet. So, being the good friends we were, Burt and I helped build Hoppy a "habitat" in Burt's backyard (aka a hole in the ground filled with water and equipped with a miniature Barbie chair and table). Yeah, spoiler alert: An open-topped hole is *not* an excellent place to keep your pet toad, no matter how many dead flies you put in there.

"Uh, okay," Burt croaked out. "But, you know, I think grass kinda grew over that spot, and I'm pretty sure he isn't—"

Anna cut him off with a laugh. "Just kidding, guys," she said. "How about a video game?"

Burt pointed to the far wall. "Awesome! Take your pick."

Anna headed over to the game shelf, and I had another sudden flashback of her at four, scaling the dresser in her bedroom to get the toy pony on top—and bringing the whole thing crashing down and trapping her underneath it. Luckily, her bed broke the fall, or Anna would have been a pancake. Burt, Anna, and I must've spent a good half hour trying to push that thing back up to free her before we finally caved and got her mom.

Anna flipped through boxes, stopping at one.

"Cool! You've got *Dr. Fantastic's Seven Levels of Doom!*" She yanked the disc from its case and waved it in the air. "Let's play this!"

And if that wasn't cool enough . . .

"Holy cow!" Burt yelled. He was bouncing up and down on his blue beanbag chair like a Mexican jumping bean. (Yeah, I had an encounter with one of those in fourth grade too. Super easy to swallow, like a pill. They don't keep hopping in your belly though, which was sort of a letdown.)

"Holy cow! You're going to reach the seventh level of

doom!" Burt pointed at the television screen. Dr. Fantastic's laser beamed purple across the dark night sky.

Burt and I have never made it to the seventh level. We've gotten to the sixth once. But that was purely by accident. Only happened 'cause we were wrestling over the clicker and pushed something by mistake. We tried to re-create that scene about a thousand times at least, including the headlock and attempted wedgie. But we never could figure out what we pushed or in what combination to ever do it again.

"Holy cow!" Burt yelled.

Anna tossed her ponytail to one side and it bounced on her right shoulder. "It's no big deal. I've done it, like, a million times before." She twisted her body left and right and pressed a couple of buttons. "Take that, Lord Dracor!"

"Holy cow!" It was Burt, still having a cow. "You're going to defeat Lord Dracor. I've never seen anyone defeat Lord Dracor!" His voice did that high-pitched squeak thingy like when he'd called me earlier.

"It's easy," Anna said, turning the joystick. "All you need is the secret ring of doom."

She swung the joystick again, and suddenly Lord Dracor evaporated in a massive ball of fire. Then the entire screen swirled with exploding stars of yellow, orange, and red, and the television flashed white and black.

"The Fantastic Screen of Death." Burt collapsed in his chair and put his arm across his head. His mouth flopped open and the back of his neatly combed hair popped straight up. "I've only heard about that. Never thought I'd live to see it. I thought it was just urban legend."

Anna set down her remote with a huge smile. "Eh, I can show you how if you guys want."

"Well, duh," said Burt.

"Double duh," I added.

"Oh!" Anna said. "Do you guys like the comics?"

Do we like the comics? Hello! If Burt and I had access to every tool in Dr. Fantastic's lab, we couldn't create anyone cooler than Anna.

"'Cause you aren't gonna believe what I found in the base thrift shop in Italy." She paused and raised her eyebrows dramatically. "A *whole box* of vintage *Dr. Fantastic*s . . . even the very first edition."

"The first edition!" Burt popped back up again, slapping down his crazy hair with both hands. "You mean the one where Dr. Fantastic creates the beginnings of the alien atmosphere and launches his inaugural Star Climber into space?"

"Yeah. That one. Mom says it'll be worth something

someday." Anna bunched her lips together. "I'm not too sure though, since some kid named Edgar wrote his name all over the front in red Sharpie."

"Bummer," Burt said.

"Yeah, but it's still fun to read! You guys can come over anytime and check the whole collection out. Well, once I find them. They're still in a box somewhere. Could take a couple of years, ha-ha." She crinkled her nose in the most adorable way and smiled.

"Sounds cool to me," I said. I didn't care if it took a hundred years. I'd be happy to wait, just for the chance to hang out with Anna more.

When I got back to my room that evening, Tomy was dancing in a shower of glitter. So I guess that meant I'd nailed step four.

Finally!

Good-bye, comfort zone!

16

AFTER ANNA MOVED AWAY, JOSH KINDA SLID IN and took her place as amigo number three in our group. He was new to the neighborhood, and Burt's mom had promised Mr. and Mrs. Chan there were lots of kids around when she sold them the house. (In fact, I'm pretty sure his mom told my parents the same thing when we moved to the 'hood. I guess you could say Burt is one of Mrs. Miller's best marketing tools.)

So, it just seemed sort of logical (if not a little risky) to bring Anna to Josh's pool.

As we walked out the basement door to Josh's patio, I wondered if we should issue some sort of warning to Anna. You know, just in case Josh was standing there with his hand tucked under his armpit in greeting.

Luckily, he was already in the pool.

Josh's wet head popped out of the water in the shallow end. He rubbed his eyes and looked at Burt. Me. And then Anna.

"Yo, Josh," Burt said. "This is Anna."

"Yo!" Josh answered. Then he let out a funny snort and looked at each of us again. Uh-oh.

"Well," he said. "What are you waiting for? Somersault challenge!" He dove under the water and started spinning—then resurfaced, shook his hair, and said, "Four! Beat that, ha!"

Before Burt and I could even get our shoes off, Anna shouted, "You're on!" She dropped her things, jumped into the pool next to Josh, and started spinning.

"Six!" she said, popping to the surface with a splash.

Josh's mouth flopped open.

"Oh yeah?" Burt said, tossing his gear on a chair and jumping in the pool. "Nobody beats me at the handstand competition!"

Well, except Anna.

I slipped into the pool and watched in awe as Anna outlasted Burt doing underwater handstands by a full ten seconds. Every. Single. Time. Burt looked even more confused than Josh.

"Okay," he said, climbing from the pool and standing at the edge with his hands on his hips. "I've got it . . . cannonball contest!"

"Yes!" Josh said, joining him. "C'mon, Farley. You're our not-so-secret weapon!"

Yeah, not a chance. "I'm good!" I said, and flopped onto my back.

Anna, though, she climbed to the edge of the pool and cannonballed in with such force she actually created a wave. Poor Tomy would never forgive me for leaving him at home.

"Holy cow," Burt said.

"How'd she do that?" Josh muttered.

But see, that was the great thing about Anna. There had always been a whole lot more to her than what you'd expect. Like that time in first grade she taught herself a handful of phrases in French so she could make our new classmate from Montreal feel welcome. Or yesterday, when we all played hoops together in her driveway and she didn't laugh when the ball bounced off the backboard and whacked me in the face. Instead, she showed me how to angle my shot and . . . *swish!*

We floated around for a while longer, until it was time to assemble in our usual post-swim position around the molded plastic table to dry off, a soda bottle between us. Josh handed out the cups. One for me, one for Burt, and one for Anna. He silently unscrewed the top and poured. Burt and I looked at each other. There was no way this could turn out well. Not with that stupid grin on Josh's face.

Josh was just about to open his mouth when there was a rustle in the bushes. In a flash, Sprinkles skidded across the patio and dumped something at his feet. Josh reached down and grinned even more.

"Hey, Fartley," he said, swinging a limp green lizard by its limp green tail over the table. "Dare you." He smacked his lips together and said, "Mmmmmmmm . . ." The lizard came to life, and its head twitched.

"Gross!" Burt said, jolting back.

Josh laughed. "Double dog," he said. "Triple dog!" He inched the disgusting thing closer to my face. "Can't be any worse than that grasshopper. Or the cricket."

Burt snorted.

"Geez, Josh. I'm not in fourth grade anymore!" I stared straight ahead and not at Anna sitting next to me, who must've thought I'd spent the last five years turning myself into a complete pig. Not exactly an upgrade from Buzz Lightyear.

"Suit yourself," Josh said, flinging the miniature reptile back into the bushes. He wiped his hands on his pants, grabbed his cup, and raised it in the air.

"Well?" he said, nodding like an out-of-control bobblehead. Burt and I didn't move. We should have known it was too much to hope that Josh could act normal for more than one hour. Not with his track record. Next he'd be explaining how it is scientifically possible, albeit dangerous (as I am well aware), to light a fart. He might even offer to have me demonstrate.

"Well, what?" Anna said, looking back and forth between me, Josh, and Burt.

"Oh geez, Josh. No," Burt said. He shook his head real fast, and little splats of water zinged me in the face.

"No what?" Anna asked. "Somebody better tell me!"

"Nothing!" Burt said.

"Oh, c'mon," Anna said.

"You see," Josh said with a dumb fat grin on his face. "We've got this little contest thing."

"Another contest?" Anna said. "I'm in!"

"Oh, Josh, you wouldn't." Burt groaned. He shimmied down in his chair, hand on his forehead.

"Well, you'd better now," Anna said. "Whatever it is."

Josh smirked, nodded, and brought the cup to his lips. Down the hatch in one swig.

Buuuuuuurrrrrppp!

He laughed. "Go ahead, boys."

Burt and I silently chugged our sodas.

Buuurrrrrpppp! went Burt.

Burp, went New Farley, hand over mouth. "Excuse me," I said. Old Farley winced.

Josh said, "What was that, Fartley?"

I looked away.

Anna looked at Josh. Anna looked at Burt. Anna looked at Old-New Farley.

Anna took her drink, placed it between her lips, and chugged it in one enormous swig, eyes pinched shut. She opened her mouth.

BUUUUUUUUUUURRRRRRRRPPPPPPPPPP!!!

I swear, the table almost shattered into a billion pieces. Birds flew from nearby trees and screeched across the cloudless summer sky. Small animals scampered underneath the shrubs. The soda bottle tipped over, and Sprite dribbled onto the patio.

"Wow!" yelled Josh. "That was amazing! She sure whooped you, Fart!"

"Farley," I said. "It's FARRR-LEY!"

Anna smiled demurely and wiped her lips.

I glanced at Burt. He was laughing so hard his face had turned bright pink and there was no noise coming from his mouth. Not a single sound. Just funny little tears squeezing from the corners of his eyes. He clutched his belly and snorted. Then he looked down in horror at his bathing suit.

"Uh-oh," he whispered. He ran to the pool and flopped in.

"Burt! You'd better not be getting pee in my pool!"

Burt peeked up over the edge, face red. He dodged back under the water, and all we saw were a few bubbles and a whoosh of blond hair floating to the surface. Then he took off with a huge kick.

Anna laughed. "You guys are the best." She gave my arm a friendly thump. "It's so cool to be back."

And for one fleeting, delusional moment, I actually thought this ridiculous plan of mine might work.

17

THE NEXT FEW DAYS WERE ACTUALLY PRETTY great—shooting hoops, hanging at Josh's pool, and then, even better—Anna said the five words Burt and I had been waiting to hear:

"I found the *Dr. Fantastic*s."

Burt and I practically raced each other to Anna's house, and there may have been a small jostling match at her front door to see who could get in first. (Me, ha! Sometimes there's an advantage to having bulk on your side.)

Anna met us in the foyer.

Her house is the exact mirror image of Burt's inside—entry with a big, tall ceiling, kitchen in the back. But her family room sits off to the left, and the living and dining rooms are off to the right. In fact, it's basically just another variation of every single house in Gentle Cove, including mine.

"C'mon in," Anna said. "The *Dr. Fantastic*s are downstairs."

Burt and I followed her into the basement, which was also just like Burt's. Except it was full of half-unpacked boxes and crumpled newspaper strewn everywhere. Made sense, I supposed, since they'd just moved here.

"'Scuse the mess," Anna said.

"No biggie," Burt answered.

Truth is, Burt and I couldn't care less about messes. I mean, once we had a contest to see who could wear the same clothes for the most days without our parents noticing and making us change. (Spoiler alert: We both lost. Parents are way more observant than we sometimes give them credit for.)

Anna stopped in a box-free clearing in the middle of the room. Leo and Al were straight ahead playing some gun battle game on a big-screen television that hung from the far wall.

"Hey, Leo. Hey, Al," Anna said. "You remember Farley and Burt?"

Leo and Al grunted in our general direction without looking back, then returned to blasting each other with on-screen lasers.

"Take that, Alpo!" the big one called Leo said.

"Oh yeah? You're going down, Leo-nard!" the equally big one called Al responded.

Anna shoved past them.

"Hey! Watch out, Ant," Al said. He craned his neck to see past Anna, and Leo blasted his avatar on-screen. "Aw man, sis! You just got me blown away." He threw his controller onto the floor. It skidded across the carpet.

"Sorry, Al," Anna said, dragging a large box to where Burt and I stood.

Leo thumped Al and pointed outside. "Hoops?" he said.

"You got it!"

"Bye, kiddies," Al said as they hulked toward the door.

Anna ignored them. Instinctively, Burt and I moved out of the way. At least now we knew enough not to accept any offers of cake (or "chocolate" bars—don't ask) from them. And we'd definitely be checking the toilet for Saran wrap before we used it too.

"Okay, here they are," Anna said. She pulled the box open. At least a couple hundred *Dr. Fantastic*s must have been stacked inside.

"Awesome!" Burt said. He grabbed the top issue and flipped it open. "I haven't read this one before!"

I took the one underneath and had a seat. Ink smudged my sweaty fingers. I wiped them on my shorts. Oops. Another candidate for the hallway hamper.

Anna grabbed a comic and sat down on the floor next to me, tucking her legs up. She smiled and put her chin on her knees.

Holy Fantastic, our shoulders were touching.

I pretended to read. Instead, I took several sneaking glances at Anna's face. Still eight freckles. Wait a minute—was that the beginning of number nine? She smelled like strawberry bubble gum. And I could now see she had the cutest ears, with tiny heart-shaped gold earrings. I wished I could sit there forever, just so I could look at her. My stomach did a bunch of flips. What was happening to me?

"That's a good one, isn't it?" Anna leaned over and pointed at the *Dr. Fantastic* on my lap. It had been open to the same page for, like, the last six hundred hours. Oh crap, and it was upside down, too.

"Huh?" I jolted. "Oh yeah, real good," I said. I turned the comic right side up and flipped the page. I could feel my cheeks burning.

Burt glanced up from his comic, inspected our almost connected shoulders, and scowled. His eyes scanned the room.

"Hey!" he said. "You have *Super Power Dance Party*!"

"Sure," Anna said. She popped up. My poor shoulder went cold and lonely. "Wanna play?"

"Yeah! I love that game," Burt said.

It was my turn to scowl at Burt.

Farley doesn't dance. New or Old. And Burt knew that.

"Hey, Fart . . . uh, ley. Farley," Burt said. He dragged out the big mat full of evil green arrows and spread it on the floor. "Wanna go first?" he said in his sweetest voice.

I narrowed my eyes. "No. After you, Squir . . . uh, Burt," I said.

Anna shoved the disc in the console and pushed play. Burt hopped on the mat and danced. Perfectly, of course. Left foot! Right foot! He was the picture of style and grace, tapping the mat in perfect time. He even gave old exercise-video Fart Lady a run for her money.

"Yes! High score!" Burt pumped his right hand in the air as the song ended. He hopped off and did a little victory dance, hands waving over his head. "Next?"

"You go," I said to Anna. Maybe if I wasted enough time we'd have to leave before poor Old Farley's turn. Maybe it would start to storm outside and the big red-headed goons would return and want their television back. At this point I'd even have been willing to eat some sponge cake if offered.

No such luck.

"You're up, Farley!" Anna said after her sweet-footed dance, the dance that had turned poor in-progress Farley into an (even bigger) quivering mess.

"Yeah, okay," I said.

I unrolled myself from the floor and stepped on the horrible mat. The music started. *Bum-bum-bum!* Burt was gonna pay for this. He smiled at me smugly from the corner, leaning all cool-like on a pile of half-unpacked boxes. I glared at him. He winked.

On the screen in front of me, directional arrows started flashing.

Crap. Was that left or right? Shoot, missed another one. Okay, that one was definitely left. Oh man, missed that stinker too.

I wished the floor would open up and swallow me. How long was this song, anyway? Four hours? A hundred years?

More arrows shot past. I was lost. Sweat began to roll between my shoulder blades. When would this ever end?

But then a Converse-clad foot stomped the mat next to me. The game *beep*ed.

Say what? I glanced to my right. Anna grinned at me.

"Sometimes it's more fun to make up your own dance! Who needs boring directions, right?" She stuck her tongue out, did an exaggerated shimmy, then spun around, crossed her arms, and pointed at me. "Go!"

"Uh, okay."

I stretched my legs and stomped, then bobbed my head like a chicken and flapped my arms.

"Ha-ha-ha, yes!" Anna said, launching into a herky-jerky version of the Running Man. Her eyebrows moved up and down in time with her arms. I laughed back and did the twist. At this point I'm pretty sure my score was zero. Maybe even minus zero, if that was at all possible. I did a few Dad-style warm-up jumps and jabs with my eyes crossed.

Anna cracked up and dabbed, bonking herself in the head.

I made a super-serious face and ran my fingers dramatically over my eyes in V shapes like I saw on YouTube once.

Anna crouched, facing me, and mirrored my move. And we kept right on going until we were both howling with laughter and the song ended.

"That was awesome, Farley!" Anna said, breathless. "Even funnier than the time you tied your shoelaces together on purpose in kindergarten. Penguin Farley . . ." She put her arms to her sides, wobbled back and forth, and gave me a friendly tap on the arm, just like at Josh's pool. Burt grumbled.

"Oh yeah? Not as funny as that time you turned *your* shoelaces into a crown and declared yourself the Queen of England. *I think I'll have a spot of tea with my Goldfish!*" I said in a high-pitched voice, and gave her a friendly tap back.

Burt grumbled even more. His eyes turned into blue slits.

"I'm the lead singer in a band," he said, adjusting his shirt and leaning one elbow on the boxes.

"Yeah?" Anna said. "That's cool. I play keyboard! Maybe I could jam with you sometime."

"I'm in the band too," I said. "I play guitar."

"*Toy* guitar," Burt said under his breath. I narrowed my eyes back at him.

"Or is it air guitar?" I started dancing again, swinging my arm wildly over my imaginary instrument, while Burt scowled and Anna doubled over laughing.

I glanced at Burt and gave him a sly Burt-style wink.

Ha.

Take that, *lead singer*.

18

OKAY, I REALIZE I HAVEN'T MENTIONED TOMY IN a while. Sorry. Got a little distracted with the whole Anna thing. I guess crushes will do that to a person. In a way, it's too bad I'm never leaving my room again to investigate this *phenomenon* (Word of the Week #27, meaning observable fact) further. Because it was kind of a fun distraction.

While it lasted, of course.

But Tomy was still in my room, swinging in the underpants hammock—and I wasn't going to get rid of him if I kept ignoring him (and the next step).

I sat at my computer.

Tomy poked his golden curls through one of the underpants hammock leg holes. "Aloha!" He swung back and forth. "Are you ready to continue your journey?"

"Actually," I said. "I'd much rather chill. I haven't

read *War and Peace*, and I'm completely stumped on how to be a hero. But onward, I guess."

"Excellent decision . . . ," Tomy began. I sniffed the air and coughed, cutting him short.

"What is that smell?"

"Smell?" Tomy sat up and sniffed. "Right on! It's the smell of the surf." He grabbed a bottle from behind his hammock and held it in the air. He squirted a little something into his hand and rubbed it on his neck. "Ahhhh, I've missed this. . . ."

"The surf? What are you talking about?" I leaned in closer. "Wait a minute!" I snatched the bottle and read the label:

> *Stink B'Gone, Limited-Edition Ocean*
> *Breeze Scent*
> *For combatting life's smellier moments . . .*

"This is air freshener!" I said, setting the bottle back down with a *thump*. "Where did you get this?"

"In the room down the hall. A most excellent find! You should try some, dude. Nothing soothes the soul like salty ocean air. . . ." He leaned back, closed his eyes, and started swinging back and forth. I could feel my pulse quickening.

"What do you mean, *down the hall*? You're not supposed to leave this room without me!" I said. "What if someone saw you?"

"I'm sorry," Tomy said. "But what choice did I have? It's totally boring in here. We never hang together anymore." He made a sad face and rubbed fake tears from his eyes. "And, dude, if we're being all real, it smells like a dead fish in here."

I stared at Tomy in disbelief.

"YOU ARE SITTING IN MY UNDERPANTS!!!" I slapped my forehead. Tomy sat up and squirted a fine mist of Stink B'Gone directly into my face.

"You are welcome," he said.

I grumbled.

"Oh! And that's not the only awesome thing," Tomy continued. "I found an ocean, too . . . with *waves!* Can you believe it? Why would you hide this from me!?"

"Huh?" I said. "There's no ocean in there. There's just a bathroom. . . . Oh no! Wait a minute. Why are you wet? Please tell me you didn't . . ."

"If only there'd been more time," Tomy mused. "I didn't even get to try the Rodeo Flip. . . ."

I left Tomy swinging in the hammock and thundered down the hallway, straight into my parents' bathroom. I stopped dead in my tracks.

Water was splattered everywhere: the floor, the walls, the mirror. Little droplets clung to the ceiling and light fixtures and dribbled down the windowpane. The bathtub was filled to the brim, and the faucet and jets were going full blast. I quickly cranked the water off before the house flooded and made a run for the towel closet.

I promptly stepped in a puddle and slipped on my butt.

"Oof!" I yelled, rubbing my backside. Floor tiles are *hard*.

"Farley?" Mom's voice echoed up the stairs. "Are you okay up there? What are you doing?"

"Yes, Mom," I hollered back, wincing. She sure has excellent hearing for someone who never seems to register any of my requests for new video games. "Just bumped my toe."

"On what? That sounded like more than a toe. Where are you, anyway? Did I hear water running?"

"Yeah, I'm, uh . . . taking a bath," I shouted.

Mom didn't answer. So I got back to work throwing towels on all the puddles until it looked kinda like a beach in there—after a hurricane hit.

Someone cleared their throat in the doorway.

I jumped about half a mile.

"Oh!" I said. "Mom."

She cocked her head to the side. "Is there something

wrong with taking a bath in your *own* bathroom? And when did you even start taking baths?"

"Yeah, well . . ." My face got hot. "It's just . . . um, my bathtub is kind of small. And it doesn't have the cool jets, and, you know, sometimes I'm just in a mood to relax. Ahhhhhhh . . ." I smiled and held out my arms.

"Is that why you used all of my bath salts?" She pointed at an empty jar, tipped sideways at the edge of the tub. My face turned red. *Tomy.*

"I'm sorry," I muttered. "I won't do it again."

"Okay, Farley," she said. "But you only need one scoop. And next time it would be nice if you asked first."

"I will. Promise."

"I'll leave you to it, then. Enjoy your bath," Mom said as she turned and closed the door behind her. "And don't forget to clean up after yourself!"

Phew. That was a close call.

And now I guess I had to take a bath. Which, truth be told, did sound rather relaxing.

Until I lowered myself into it and had to bite back a scream.

I should have known Tomy would fill it with *cold* water.

I knew then I'd better click that scroll so I could get him out of my house ASAP.

19

Step Five: Cast Aside the "Haters"!
On your path to a new you, you will encounter
others who choose to stand in your way.
These people may be your friends, they may be
coworkers, or they may be family. They may
even have your best interests at heart. But they
will slow you down, either because they benefit
from your failure or because they fear your
success. Do not let them do it! Do not let these
people pull you down! When you encounter a
hater, remind yourself, "I am bigger than the
challenges around me! I can rise to the occasion!"

I left Tomy in my room that night with a strict
warning for the love of all things good NOT TO GO

ANYWHERE and headed to Josh's for band practice. Of course, Tomy tried to jump in my hoodie, but there was no way I was hauling around a tiny pest that smelled like the bathroom after Grandpa uses it for an hour. Not worth the risk.

Practice was in Josh's garage, because that's where the drums were set up. According to Mr. Chan, Sprinkles is not a big fan of rock and roll. It was a little hot out there, so we cracked the garage door open to let in some air. And even better, we'd found another cool song on my guitar— "Sweet Home Alabama." Even though it's also a thousand years old and we don't live anywhere near Alabama, it's pretty good. We downloaded the lyrics too, so now Burt had something to scream into his Coca-Cola.

"So," Burt said as we got ready to jam. "What we really need is a *gig*."

"A gig?" I stopped fake-tuning my guitar and gulped. It was one thing playing a toy in Josh's garage. It was a whole different thing playing in front of other people. "I don't know about that. . . ."

"Hmm," Josh said. "No, Burt is right. We need a gig! A *paying* gig . . ." He picked at a faded yellow sticker on his shiny gold cymbal as he talked. Every piece of Josh's drum set sports a color-coded sticker in a different shape, stuck there by his music teacher as a learning guide. They kinda lack street cred, though, so Josh had been peeling them off bit by bit.

"So . . ." Josh flicked a sticker piece onto the cement garage floor. "How about your bar mitzvah, Burt?"

"Yeah, but that's, like, a whole year away," Burt said. "We need a gig *now*."

"Actually," I said. "The bar mitzvah sounds perfect!"

By then maybe I would own a real guitar. Or at the very least, Burt would have completely forgotten about this whole band idea. Sort of like the way he abandoned the "Extreme Tricycling" thing in preschool when he discovered you couldn't actually get any air riding off the curb at top speed. Just bruises.

Josh tapped his cymbal with a drumstick. *Ding, ding, ding.* He and Burt kept right on discussing venues.

"Your mom's company picnic?" Burt said.

"Nope," Josh said. "Already had it last week."

"Humph. Well, there's got to be something." Burt scratched his chin. "Party?"

Josh tapped the sticks faster, and then all at once they both looked at me.

"Farley!" Burt said. "Your birthday party!"

"Yeah!" Josh said. "Your party's next month, right?"

"Yeah," I said, swallowing hard. "It is. In two weeks, actually."

"So, can we play your party?" Burt asked.

"Think your parents will pay us?" Josh said.

"Pay us? Do you really need to ask?" I said. "My dad won't even pay for his own haircuts. Mom does them. And I still get only five dollars for allowance."

"Right. Guess not." Josh twirled the drumsticks in front of his face. "But the publicity will be good, right? It could lead to a paying gig, right?"

"Uh, sure," I said. A paying gig at the Sunrise Retirement Village if Great-Aunt Alice showed up. "You never know. It could, I guess."

"Cool," said Burt. "Farley's party it is. Let's jam!"

Before I could say another word, Josh raised his drumstick.

"A one! A two! A one, two, three!" He tapped the yellow triangle, then the blue square, then what was left of the red rectangle. I flipped my guitar's on switch, stomach churning. I did *not* have a good feeling about this. . . .

Burt cradled his soda bottle between two hands and closed his eyes.

Bum-bum-de-dum, bum-bum-de-dum, the guitar hummed.

"Big wheels keep on turnin'," Burt crooned. "Carry me home to see my can . . ."

"It's 'kin,' Burt, 'kin'!" Josh yelled over the music. "Carry me home to see my kin! You know, like family."

"Yeah, okay, whatever, Josh," Burt said. He went back to singing. He did the leg kick like last time. His "signature move." Said we should all think of one.

Josh stomped his foot on the bass drum. *Bong. Bong. Bong!*

"Check out my signature move!" he said, and twirled the drumstick in the air. "The fans will go *wild*!"

"Oh yeah? Anna totally loved this one!" I raised my arm over my head, then did the little finger sweep across my eyes like in my crazy dance.

Burt stopped shouting into his soda bottle.

"Anna? What do you mean, *Anna* loved that one?" He raised an eyebrow. Josh's drumsticks hovered midair. My miniature guitar hung limp from my neck, still playing the chorus over and over, red lights blinking on the black frets.

"Nothing," I said. "I was just saying . . . Never mind. Forget it."

Burt snorted. "Sure, I'll forget it. It was a pretty stupid thing to say anyway."

"Hey! What's that supposed to mean?" I asked.

"C'mon, Fart. Be serious, now," Burt said.

"I am serious."

"So am I," Burt said. "If Anna likes any move, it'll be this one."

He pumped his soda bottle in the air three times and made some ridiculous howling noise.

"Really?" I said, face growing hot. "Why not this?" I did the arm-swing finger sweep again with a little extra flair.

"Why not . . . ?" Burt rolled his eyes.

I glared at him. "Well? *Why not?*"

As if I even needed to ask. I knew what Burt was thinking. *Just go ahead and say it, Burt. Say it!*

"Well . . . she was my friend first!" Burt said instead.

"By, like, five minutes!" I said. "Besides, you can't call dibs on a girl. Who made you Napoléon anyway?"

"Huh?" Burt said. "What are you even talking about? Who?"

Okay, so maybe I hadn't quite made it past the first page of *War and Peace*. But I did read the back cover. Twice.

"Napoléon," I snorted out. "Stupid little Emperor of France."

"Whatever, Fart," Burt said. "Anna's my neighbor, so I can show her my moves whenever I want. I don't need your permission."

I cranked the guitar off. "Oh yeah? She says I'm funny!"

"Funny-looking," Burt said, and puffed out his cheeks. "Better than a squirt pants!"

Josh cracked up.

Burt raised his soda bottle again and hurled it through the air. *Whack!* It popped me on the head.

"Ow!" I rubbed my offended melon, set my toy guitar on the floor, pushed Burt down, and sat on him.

"Ack, gack, ack!" He squirmed and flailed helplessly under the bulk of Old Farley.

"Take it back!" I said.

"No!" Burt said. His voice squeaked like a balloon with the air being squeezed out of it.

I shimmied up his chest.

"Take it back or I'm letting one rip right in your face!" I said.

"Gross! You wouldn't!"

I wiggled closer to the perfectly sculpted Burt snot-locker.

"And I had beans for dinner last night!" I said.

"Aghh!!!" Burt gurgled.

Josh laughed even harder.

"You two are doomed anyway. Wait till she sees this move." He twirled the drumstick in his right hand over his head like a baton, then tossed it in the air, caught it, and banged the cymbals.

"Take that, losers," he said.

Burt took advantage of the momentary distraction to knock me on my back. I flailed around like a beached whale. Burt jumped up, doing that stupid fist pump, and shouted, "Dibs!"

I rolled over to heave myself up, and that's when I saw them peeking beneath the garage door—

A pair of tie-dyed Converse.

Josh's eyes followed my gaze, then grew wide. He pushed the button next to the kitchen door, and the garage door slid open. Anna stood on the other side, her pool bag slung over her shoulder, a small frown on her face.

Oh no. How long had she been standing there?

She looked at Josh, then Burt, then me, still sprawled on the floor. I tried to scramble to my feet and say something, but before I could open my mouth, Anna spoke.

"I'm a person, you know," she said. "Not a *Dr. Fantastic* you get to wrestle over."

And with that she turned around and left.

20

"HEY, FAR," DAD SAID, PEERING OVER HIS BOILED egg at breakfast the next morning. "They had a special on climbing wall tickets yesterday at the gym, so I picked up a couple. Thought maybe you'd like to take Burt along today."

Humph. Burt. No, thanks. I still couldn't get that hurt look on Anna's face from last night out of my head. I didn't get it. Why wasn't she happy we were all fighting over her?

"I think I'd rather go alone," I said. I was a solo act now. The Farley Project. I chewed my slimy prune as fast as I could and washed it down with a swig of orange juice. *Gak!*

Dad's lips pursed together. "They're only good for today. I don't want to waste them. They were five dollars each. Five dollars," he said with emphasis, holding five long fingers in the air.

Oh boy.

"Sorry, Dad. Burt's, uh, busy today."

"Well, what about your other pal, there? That Chan kid?" Dad said.

"He's busy too."

"Well, there must be someone you can bring along," Dad said. "I'm not wasting that ticket."

Would a miniature self-help expert in my hood count?

"Ooh!" Mom said. "I know! Why don't you bring Anna?"

"Uhhhh . . . ," I stammered. That was the worst idea yet. The way Anna walked away from Josh's, I was quite certain she wanted absolutely nothing to do with me. Or any of us.

"Yes," Mom continued. "Saw her mom the other day at sewing club. Said how happy Anna was to be back in town with Far and his buddies. I'll give her a call!"

Wait, what?

Mom didn't even bother to wait for an answer, just popped right up from her seat and grabbed the phone from the kitchen wall. She twirled the white cord around her finger and tapped her foot on the tile floor.

"Yes! Hi, Jenny," she said. "It's Meg." Pause. "Yes, doing

well too. Anyway, I was calling to see if Anna happened to be free today. Maybe she'd like to join Farley at the climbing wall at Dave's gym?"

Mom twirled her whole body around in the white cord, then unwound herself like a spinning top. She did this three more times while she listened and loaded that earpiece up with more orange goo.

"Oh!" she said. "Excellent! Farley will be so pleased."

My cheeks involuntarily turned red. I covered them with my hands. What did my mom think she was doing?

"He and Dave will pick Anna up in a half hour or so. Great! Okay, bye." She set the phone back in the cradle.

"Good news, Far. Anna's free!"

Anna didn't say much on the car ride to the gym, or when we got hooked into our climbing gear, or when we scaled the rock wall. It was pretty clear her mom had accepted this invitation without actually asking Anna first.

And now, as we hung on to the grips on the top of the wall, still not speaking, what she'd said yesterday kept looping through my head:

I'm a person. . . . I'm a person. . . . I'm a person.

What did that even mean?

I thought maybe I could fix things if I lightened them up just a bit. So I pushed myself back from the climbing wall, flailed my legs and arms around, crossed my eyes, and made monkey noises.

Anna didn't even crack a smile.

My cheeks grew hot, and I pressed myself back to the wall, feeling like a complete fool—no, a disgusting prune-filled piñata wrapped up in string. What was I doing? This was exactly the Farley I'd been trying to erase. The one who'd been covering up the real Farley under all those layers, the one trying to escape . . .

Oh.

And that's when it hit me.

I'm a *person.* . . .

"I'm sorry," I said, quietly at first, then a little louder. "I'm sorry, Anna."

"Excuse me?" Anna kept staring at the climbing wall.

"About last night," I said. My throat was dry, and my tongue felt huge in my mouth. "About that dumb wrestling match me and Burt were having."

Anna just made a weird grunting noise.

I swallowed hard and kept talking. "We do dumb stuff like that all the time. Everything's a competition with us. We once fought for ten minutes over who got to push an elevator button and missed the elevator, like, twenty times. It's stupid. I don't know why we do it."

"It is stupid," Anna said.

"I know. I'm sorry," I said again. "We didn't mean it, and we sure didn't mean to hurt your feelings." I paused and took a deep breath. "But I get why you were mad."

"You do?" Anna turned her head toward me. She was biting her lower lip.

"Yeah," I said. "Because . . . Because I understand how you felt. I'm a person too. Only no one ever sees it. They just see this." I did the monkey-dance thing again.

A small smile crept across Anna's cheeks, and I waited for her to start laughing at me. But . . . she didn't.

"I see it," she said softly.

Oh, cowabunga! My heart did about eight hundred thousand flips. "Really?"

Anna nodded. "Really."

I tried to think of something brilliant to say, but my brain was stuck on *I see it.*

Thankfully, Kev broke the silence.

"Hey, you kids ready up there yet?" he shouted from the mat below. I'd kind of forgotten he was down there. He and another gym guy named Rob gave our ropes a little tug. (Apparently to work at the Middleford Health Club all you need to have is really big muscles, the ability to fit in a tank top, and a three-letter name.)

"Ready for what?" Anna asked.

"The best part," I said. "We're going to fly!"

"Fly how?"

"Just do what I do. You ready?"

Anna nodded.

"Ready!" I shouted.

Kev and Rob gave our ropes some slack, and I pushed off the wall, Anna right behind me. We bounced down the side. Anna squealed with glee and my heart did another funny little flip. I barely even noticed Rob and Kev unhitching us from our harnesses. I actually jumped when mine fell to the floor, buckles rattling.

"Thank you. That was the best," Anna said, and out of nowhere she gave me a big hug. "What next?"

I stood there all red-faced and stupid-like, poking my right foot into the blue floor mat. I tried to say something, but all that came out was "*Farg, gurgle, urble, oog.*"

A goofy laugh came from Kev's direction. "Hey, dude," he said. "Juice bar. On the second level." He pointed up toward the glass window and nodded.

"*Farg, gurgle, uh* . . . Thanks, Kev," I sputtered.

"Don't mention it, dude," he said with a wink and a *thud* to my arm. "Good luck!"

Anna and I walked up the carpeted gym stairs to the juice bar. It sits alongside another glass wall overlooking the indoor tennis courts. We each sat on one of the tall black and silver stools and took a look at the menu board above the stainless-steel juicing machines.

A girl wearing a "Kim" name tag came out a back door and slid in front of us. Okay, did anyone here have a four-letter name? Seriously. What was up with this place? They must have an incredibly short application form.

"What can I get ya kids?" she said.

"Hmmm," Anna said. She pushed a red curl off her dewy forehead. "How about a strawberry-banana smoothie."

"You got it," Kim said. "And you, big fella?"

Prune and rice cake blend, perhaps? "I think I'll have the same," I said.

"Good deal." Kim grabbed a huge scoop of ice and dropped it in a blender, then tossed in a handful of strawberries and two bananas. With the push of a button, the mixture spun and screeched until it was a whirl of pink. Kim pressed the button again and poured the thick goop into two plastic cups.

"Here ya go," she said, sliding the smoothies in front of Anna and me. "That'll be eight dollars."

Uh-oh. I gave Kim a blank stare. I wondered if she'd fall for the innocent smile.

Nope.

I shrugged instead.

"You got a membership here?" she asked. She leaned her elbows on the bar and cracked her gum.

"Yeah, my dad. David Turner," I said.

"No problem, then," Kim said. "Why didn't you say so? We'll put it on his account. Just sign here." She ripped a piece of paper from the register and handed it to me with a blue pen. There was a line for a tip. What was acceptable? I didn't want to look cheap. Twenty bucks sounded good. I signed and gulped. Dad would be thrilled.

"Thanks!" Kim said brightly. "Come back anytime!" She disappeared behind a narrow door.

I picked up my plastic cup. The outside was all sweaty from the cold ice. It slipped around in my hand as I took a small sip.

"This was fun," Anna said. "Definitely way cooler than that thing we used to climb at the playground in preschool."

"Yeah, especially since Calvin Peterson isn't chasing us up it, waving that toy bus over his head and shouting, 'I'm gonna get you!'"

Anna laughed. "Whatever happened to him anyway?"

"Eh," I said. "He's still around. Doesn't try to hit people with toy buses anymore. More into building computers and gaming and stuff."

"I guess people change, huh?"

I nodded.

"Well," Anna said. "I'm just glad you haven't."

My heart sank.

"Don't get me wrong!" Anna said quickly, as though she could read the disappointment on my face. "Of course you totally have. I mean, I haven't seen you in a Buzz Lightyear costume once since I got back. . . ."

I couldn't stop the laugh that burst out of my mouth.

"That's only because my mom set fire to it in the backyard once I finally took it off," I said. "Told me it was for the good of humanity, or something like that."

Anna snort-laughed. "See?" she said. "That's what I mean. You're different, but you're still the Farley I remember. The one who was always fun to be around. It's nice. I was kind of worried everyone would have changed so much while I was gone, I wouldn't have any friends here anymore. A lot can happen in five years."

"But why wouldn't anybody want to be friends with you?" I said. I concentrated real hard on my smoothie. There were a million little strawberry seeds floating around in there. I wondered if I could count them all. "You're one of the coolest people I know."

"That's nice of you to say, but it's not always easy," Anna said.

"What do you mean?"

"I mean, moving all the time," she said. "We've actually lived in three places since we last lived here. Sometimes it's hard to fit in, especially when everyone already knows each other. And it's not like this doesn't stand out." She rolled her eyes and pointed at her head. "Cue the clown jokes."

"Well, I think you have the prettiest hair I've ever seen," I said, almost a whisper.

"Thanks." Anna gently touched my arm. My smoothie melted instantly. "And thanks for everything . . . up there, too." She nodded toward the climbing wall.

"I guess that was a pretty good monkey impression, wasn't it?" I said, cheeks flushing.

"You know what I mean."

"Yeah." I nodded. "I know what you mean. And thank you, too."

Anna was quiet, but she smiled. I smiled too.

"So," I said. "Are you, uh, going to have to move again?" My voice did that involuntary cracking thing, and I tried very hard not to keep turning the color of my smoothie. (Spoiler alert: The harder you try, the more you blush. Life really isn't fair.)

"Actually, no. My dad just retired."

"Retired? I didn't think your dad was that old." I tried to picture the last time I saw Colonel Murphy. I mean, he was bald, but I'm pretty sure that's just because the air force shaved all his hair off or something. He was definitely not Grandpa-Andrew-false-teeth-old.

"I dunno," Anna said. "Just dad aged. Fortysomething."

"Huh. That's like my dad. But he's not retired. In fact, he's always complaining he'll never retire. Till he's, like, a hundred." Actually, probably a hundred and one now that I'd added twenty-eight bucks to his Middleford Health Club tab.

"Oh, my dad works in an office now. He's only retired from the air force. They let you do that after twenty years. Mom said she was sick of moving around. Wanted us to stay somewhere for once."

"Oh," I said. *Way to go, Farley!* I tried to come up with something more meaningful to say, like Tomy.

"Well, it is always good to find one's center," I said, and sucked down a huge gulp of smoothie. Anna blinked a couple of times, then nodded.

"Yeah," she said. "Yeah. You're right. I like it here. I'm glad we don't have to move again."

"Yeah, me too."

Anna looked around the room. "So, what else are you into these days?" she asked. "Besides climbing, I mean."

I thought about this a minute while Anna smiled. And before I realized it, something else happened— something strange and surprising.

I relaxed. It was like I could actually talk to Anna— without worrying that she'd laugh at me. Just *with* me.

And like floating down the side of the rock wall, I found myself effortlessly telling her everything from how much I hate long division to my favorite part of a muffin (the cinnamony top) to my secret dream of exploring outer space all the way to the edge of the galaxy. And maybe even beyond.

"Like Dr. Fantastic?" she said. "Or Buzz Lightyear?"

"Sort of," I said. "But more like a real astronaut. You know, the kind that collects samples from Mars and studies moon rocks and stuff."

I leaned forward and took another big chug of smoothie. I couldn't believe I'd said that out loud. I'd never told anyone that. Ever. Not even Burt. Face it, I'm not exactly the kind of guy you picture in an astronaut suit, unless it's Halloween.

"Yeah?" Anna said. "I think that would be really cool."

"You think so?"

"Definitely," she said. "Just don't forget about all us little earthlings when you're a famous space explorer." She gave my arm a tap.

"Okay, I won't." I took another cool smoothie sip. But it only made my insides feel even warmer. "I'll name the first star I discover after you."

"It'd better be a red one," she said, and we both laughed.

I wished this day wouldn't end.

But just like bouncing down the climbing wall, you're going to hit the mat sooner or later. Out of the corner of my eye, I spotted Middleford Health Club member David Turner striding briskly toward the juice bar. His eyebrows furrowed as he spied the four-dollar drink in my hand. Four dollars. Times two. Plus tip. Uh-oh. I squeezed the cup and the plastic cracked. Then I looked at Anna's sweet face and she smiled. I smiled back. A big smile.

There was nothing that could take this moment away from me.

Not the giant gravitational pull of earth.

Not Dad.

Not anything.

Or so I thought.

21

WE WERE GOING TO DO IT. THIS TIME ME AND
Dad were actually going to do it. I could see Burt's house,
and it was close. So close I could read the little white letters spelling "Miller" on his shiny black mailbox.

"Farley! Keep up the pace! You've got it! You've got
it!" Dad slapped my back. "See! You're going to make it!"

I kept my legs moving and nodded. I wasn't wasting my breath speaking. Not with the finish line in sight.
Right there. Straight ahead. My feet pushed off the pavement. It was like I was airborne. Flying. I was Astronaut
Farley, gliding across the surface of the moon.

One foot . . . in front of the other . . .

Lawn mowers rattled; neighbors waved.

One foot . . . in front of the other . . .

Little kids laughed, scratched chalk drawings on the sidewalks.

One foot . . . in front of the other, and . . .

I was in front of Burt's house! I slowed down and jogged in place, wiping beads of sweat from my forehead. I took a few Dad-style Rocky jabs at the Miller mailbox. I sucked in my gut and pointed a couple of Rocky jabs at hater Burt's bedroom. I'd show him!

"Farley!" Dad held up his right hand in the air. "High five!"

I slapped Dad's hand. I felt like dancing right there in the middle of the sidewalk. If I'd had the energy, that was. *Go, Farley! Go, Farley! Go, Farley!* This was the best moment. Ever.

I did it!

Behind me, a basketball bounced on the pavement. I glanced over my shoulder and spotted Anna's brothers playing a game of pickup. I made a small wave, but they didn't see me.

"Water, Far?" Dad asked.

I nodded. Dad handed me the semi-chilled bottle. I took a big swig and water dripped from my chin. I watched little splats land on the sidewalk and evaporate almost immediately.

"Boy, that was a great!" Dad yammered, jogging in

place. "Nothing better than a good run to get your blood flowing!"

"Uh-huh." I handed the water back to Dad, and that's when I heard it.

Meow.

I glanced around.

Meow!

My eyes followed the sound, down the sidewalk and up the tall tree in Burt's front yard.

"Sprinkles!" It was Josh's cat, teetering on the tallest branch, eyes wide and teeth bared.

Meeeeeee-owwwww!

And right then I knew my moment had come. My chance to do something heroic.

"Don't worry, Sprinkles!" I shouted bravely. "I'll save you!"

I jogged to the base of the tree, lifted my right foot, and grunted loudly as I hoisted myself onto the bottom branch. I grabbed ahold of another branch and pulled myself up farther. Just like climbing the rock wall at Dad's gym! I extended my arm.

"Here, Sprinkles! Here, kitty, kitty!"

She hissed at me and moved farther out on the branch.

Darn cat.

I shimmied higher.

"You okay up there?" Dad shouted from the sidewalk.

"Yep!" I shouted back. *Just being a hero.*

I extended my arm toward Sprinkles again. But this time, instead of a hiss, I heard a strange ripping sound. That was followed by a whoosh of air in a very unexpected spot.

Huh?

The basketball stopped bouncing. Sprinkles stopped moving. The whole world froze. Time screeched to a halt.

Then laughter. Big laughter. Riotous, massive howls of laughter.

"Hey, kid, your Planet of Doom is showing!" Anna's brother Al yelled. Her other brother, Leo, clutched the basketball in his left hand and pointed with his right.

I ran my hand over my "derriere" and felt the inevitable torn seam, the stretchy fabric snapped all the way back to my sides like a popped balloon. And there beneath the giant hole, the raised pattern of my *Dr. Fantastic* underpants. (Yes, Mom still buys them for me. And yes, they still make them in my size.)

The laughter got louder and louder, echoing up the street. It bounced off the brick fronts of Gentle Cove's identical houses. It slammed my head like metal baseball bats.

I held in tears. I shook. The whole mound of Farley quivered.

I knew it was a bad idea to keep wearing Dad's skinny-man running shorts. Why did I listen to him when he said not to worry about it? I didn't even have a jacket to tie around my waist like Burt did on that field trip.

I slowly lowered my leg to begin climbing down from the tree, and when I did, something else happened. Something far worse.

Rrrrriiiipppp!

The last bit of that super-futuristic stretchy fabric gave way, the waistband popped, and—*swoosh*—those ridiculous shorts sprang loose, slid down my leg, and landed in a shiny heap on the grass. Sprinkles darted from the top branch with a screech-hiss, hit the ground on all four paws, and snagged my shorts in her teeth—then ran off.

Aaaagh!

Could this get any more horrifying?

Well, what did you know—it could. There, up in the corner window, peeking from behind a set of pink lace curtains, was Anna's face, her mouth forming an O. There were Anna's big blue eyes looking down her freckle-covered nose at me, hanging from a branch in Burt's tree like a snagged balloon. In my underpants. My Planet of Doom size XXL underpants.

I was completely beat. Whooped. But I mustered up

the energy to hop down and run. I ran as fast as my stubby legs would take me. As fast as I'd ever run in all my life. And I didn't look back. Not even when I heard my dad yelling, "Hey, Farley. *Farley*. Wait up!" I just went as fast as I possibly could until I was off the street and back in my room, collapsed in a pile of sweat on my bed.

As for how the rest of my morning went, here's a snapshot:

Mom: walks in room for hundred millionth time. "Farley, are you going to stay in here forever?"

Farley: pulls blankets over head and turns away on bed.

Dad: walks in room for hundred millionth time. "Farley, get up! You can't stay in here forever!"

Farley: "Really? Watch me. Just watch me. Maybe I will."

Dad: exits room.

Farley: shoves that giant *War and Peace* pile of bricks in front of the bedroom door. That ought to keep everyone out. At least I finally found some use for that massive stack of dead trees.

Tomy: "There is no wave so high that one cannot conquer it with determination!"

Farley: has officially had enough.

I plucked that annoying pest from his underpants hammock, dropped him into my old sea monkey tank, and screwed on the top.

"I'm done."

And that, folks, is how I ended up here. In my room. Forever.

22

FARLEY ANDREW TURNER'S TOP TEN LIST OF
things to do when trapped inside one's bedroom for all
eternity, stuck with an annoying self-help master:

1. Rearrange all of the socks in your sock
    drawer. Do not accept help from self-help
    master. (He's just trying to get out.) Sort
    by size, color, use, and purpose. Do this
    seventeen times or until you fall asleep.

2. Count all of the individual yarn pieces in
    the carpet. Keep counting while you ignore
    self-help master's pleas until you reach a
    thousand or fall asleep on the floor.

3. See how long you can balance a pencil
    across the bridge of your nose while lying

in bed. Continue to hold this position as long as possible while not listening to The Online Master's advice. Or until you fall asleep.

4. Untie the laces of all the shoes in your closet, retie them, and untie again. Repeat twelve times or until you no longer hear The Online Master and fall asleep with your head on the shoe rack.

5. Try holding your breath as long as you can until The Online Master makes no sound and you pass out. Or fall asleep.

6. Pick all of the lint out from between your toes and line it up on your self-help master's "meditation cushions" until you're totally grossed out or fall asleep.

7. Hang upside down off the edge of the bed without making eye contact with your self-help master. Do this for at least an hour or until the blood rushes to your head and causes you to lose consciousness or fall asleep.

8. Wait for the exact moment that the sun streams through your window and lights up all the little specks of dust floating

through the air. Try to catch those specks of dust with your pointer finger and thumb without being distracted by your self-help master doing yoga. Continue until you catch one hundred or fall asleep.

9. Imagine all the places you are going to hide when school starts in a week: under the bed, in the closet, behind the door. Do not release self-help master. Do not stop until you fall asleep.

10. Sleep.

The doorbell chiming wakes me up. Next, footsteps. Next, knocking on my door.

"Yeah, come in," I say feebly. I rub my eyes and glance at the clock, wondering how many days have passed since my self-imposed exile began.

And . . . it's been all of two hours. Great.

The door pushes open.

There's Mom, hand resting on the doorknob. "Hi, honey," she says. "You have a visitor."

"I do?"

"Yep," she says.

"That's nice."

Mom keeps standing there. How'd she get past *War*

and Peace, anyway? Right, she's Mom. "I'm not leaving my room," I say.

"Far . . . ," she says, tapping her foot.

"Oh, all right."

I pull myself off the bed, trudge downstairs, and walk to the door.

"Yo, Fart."

"Oh, hey, Burt."

"Gee, don't get so excited to see me," he says.

"Sorry," I say. "What's up?"

Burt's got his hands behind his back. He shrugs and smiles. "It's Wednesday. Duh. Grady's. *Dr. Fantastic.* You ready to go?"

I look past Burt's shoulder at the big blue Miller-mobile rumbling in the driveway. A giant pretend Mrs. Miller is plastered on the side, leaning on a miniature house, and holding an enormous key in her right hand. The real Mrs. Miller is in the driver's seat, cell phone pressed between her ear and shoulder, hands furiously lifting and spritzing her mile-high hair. No wonder Burt smells like perfume half the time.

"Right," I say. "Sorry. I don't think so."

"Oh?" Burt's lips curl into a smirk. "Why not?"

"No reason."

Burt's hands fidget behind his back, and he chokes

back a laugh. "You lose something this morning by any chance?"

His right arm swings around, producing a short, crooked stick with my ripped running shorts dangling from the end. He waves them around and marches in place.

"I think you really need to lay off the beans, Fart," he says, and doubles over in laughter. Blood rushes to my face, and I snatch what's left of that super-futuristic stretchy stink bomb off Burt's makeshift flagpole.

"Go away," I say.

"Oh, lighten up!" Burt says with a snort.

"No, you lighten up," I grumble.

Burt chucks the stick into the bushes. "Geez, Fart. It was just a joke! And a funny one!" He laughs again and wipes a tear away from the corner of his eye.

"I . . . am . . . not . . . a . . . joke!"

"Hey, all right. Geez, calm down. When did you get so serious all of a sudden?"

I don't say anything.

Burt juts his thumb over his shoulder. "So, are you coming or not? My mom's waiting."

"Not."

"Aw, man. C'mon, Fart. You know I hate to go there alone with my mom. She's probably gonna make me stand around the bakery and hand out business cards to all the little old ladies." He frowns, but then that stupid smirk creeps across his cheeks again. "Besides, you might be able to get a needle and thread there." He points at my ripped running shorts.

Grrr . . .

"Good-bye," I say, pushing the door shut. But before I can click it in place, he picks up his foot and jams his white sneaker in the frame.

"Wait!" he says.

"What is it now?"

"Well, the Fantastics are still playing your party, right?" He smiles and nods.

I don't even dignify that with a response.

I kick Burt's foot away, slam the door, stomp back upstairs, and grab my emergency box of Twinkies off the nightstand. I stare at them long and hard. I look at that beautiful, unnaturally yellow cake and think how good it would be to just slide one out of its little plastic prison and bite off the top. My next move, the one I've perfected over a million Twinkies, would be to scoop out the delicious cream filling with my tongue. Then I'd drop the rest of that luscious, spongy cake right in the slot and devour it in one massive bite. I'm sure I could polish off all seven in T minus ten seconds, probably without even coming up for air.

Sweet, scrumptious, wonderful Twinkies. My best friends in the whole world. Always there for poor, pitiful Farley when he needs them.

Or not.

I mean, let's face it—when was the last time a Twinkie laughed at one of my jokes or told me I was cool or that I'd done a *meritorious* job on my word of the week? Maybe all they were good at was filling that empty space inside me when no one else did. Who cares if they're delicious and I love them? Maybe I don't deserve delicious things in the first place.

So I shake the box and dump all those dumb, mouth-watering cakes on the floor. Then I smash one with my right foot. The plastic wrapper pops and white cream and cake ooze out the side. I demolish another one, with even more force this time. A piece of Twinkie flies off and hits the wall. It sticks there, then slides down, leaving a trail of slimy goo in its wake.

Ha!

I can hear Tomy shouting something from his sea monkey prison, but I ignore him and jump up and down—until every last stupid yellow bit of tasty goodness is flattened on the floor and my socks are covered with the sticky remains of dead Twinkie. I look with satisfaction at the gooey mess on the carpet. Mom's gonna kill me. But who cares? Better to expire at the hands of Mom than in the halls of MMS when school starts.

I peel off my socks and hurl them in the direction of the hamper. Then I climb into bed and pull the covers over my head to await my horrible fate.

23

APPARENTLY MY PUNISHMENT FOR SQUASHING Twinkies into the floor, other than "cleaning it up myself" is to help Mom with the grocery shopping.

Even though I tried to argue that I wasn't leaving my room except for fire, flood, or other catastrophic events, Mom wasn't moved. I guess in Mom's book, Twinkie assassination falls into one of those categories.

So here I sit in the back of the minivan.

"How you doing back there, Far?" Mom asks. She pretends to adjust the mirror and looks at me. "Everything okay?"

"Yeah, sure," I say. "Everything's just grand."

I glance away and watch Middleford's quiet streets slide by in a whoosh of green and brick and winding sidewalks and black lampposts. Almost every car we pass is a minivan, like ours, with kids jammed in the back watching little televisions. Only I don't have a television back here. Dad thought that was a pointless upgrade for two thousand dollars. He got the super-studded snow tires and luggage rack instead. Lots of good those do me.

"All right," Mom says in her I'm-not-convinced voice. Thankfully, she drops the subject, and soon we're rolling into the Grady's parking lot. Mom approaches an empty spot like Josh's cat when it corners a mouse. She tentatively pulls partway in and out of the space at least fifty-seven times before finally giving up, charging straight ahead, and throwing the car into park.

"Darn tiny spaces, giant cars," she mutters while climbing out with her massive purse slung over her right arm. She stops and inspects the minivan—front left tire over the left white line, right rear tire across the right, then looks at me and shrugs.

I follow Mom through Grady's automatic front doors, taking extra care to keep my eyes pointed down. On the other side, Mom grabs a metal cart, waves over her shoulder, and clanks off toward the boiled food department.

"See ya in a minute, honey," she says, which in Mom time means about seven million hours or so. I look for something inconspicuous to do.

If you've never been in Grady's, it's one of those stores

with a little bit of everything—food, toys, movies, games, clothes, and yeah, comics. I know that new *Dr. Fantastic* is somewhere in the magazine rack at the front of the store, just waiting there in all its shiny glory. But for some reason, I can't bring myself to go over there. It's just not the same without Burt, even if he is a rotten stinking little hater.

I decide to check out the cluttered video display instead. No good videos here. Not any that Mom will let me get, at least. I'm only permitted movies in the G-minus category. I sit on a bench and try playing the statue game, holding myself as still as possible while people walk by to see if they notice me. But that's not nearly as fun without Burt either. And maybe nobody notices me anyway, whether I'm moving or not.

I lean back and stare at the red exit sign above the door. I close one eye real tight and squint, then try it with the other. Then I switch back and do the other eye, over and over. The red sign dances back and forth. That's fun for about ten seconds. I open my mouth real wide until my ears pop. I do that a thousand times and stick my tongue in and out as fast as I can until I notice some old lady by the fresh-flower display staring at me. I sit up real straight so she doesn't drop her roses and call the manager and have me tossed out. Once she's gone I try to make my nose stick shut and count the little hairs on my fingers.

Ugh. Where is Mom, and why can't she just let me have a Nintendo DS like every other kid on the planet?

After the seasons change a couple dozen times and another Ice Age passes, Mom rolls up with a cart jammed full of stuff. Finally.

"Oh, hey, Far," she says. "There you are! C'mon. You can help me at the checkout."

"Okay, Mom." I pull myself off the bench and walk with her to the register. I'm busy unloading stuff onto the conveyor belt when I hear it. That voice.

"Holy cow!"

I glance around, scan the nearby aisles, and shake my head. Must be hearing things. But no, there's that "holy cow!" again, followed by the sweetest snort-laugh I've ever heard. I drop the box of noodles in my hand.

Burt.

"Why that two-timing cad!" Mom exclaims.

"I'd say," I mutter.

I squint in the direction of the magazine rack, and there he is, a *Dr. Fantastic* clutched in his traitorous fingers, Anna at his side. She laughs at something he says and tosses her red hair around. My heart sinks.

"Of all the two-bit cheating fools!" Mom says.

"No kidding," I grumble.

"What?" Mom says. "Oh!" She shakes the flimsy paper

plastered with glossy pictures of celebrities and jams it back in the rack. "This fell out. I wasn't reading it or anything." She shuffles forward and starts punching her Grady's discount code into the keypad, still sneaking peeks at that silly magazine. She must enter that code at least six times before she finally gets it right.

"Yeah, okay, Mom," I say.

I keep watching Burt and Anna as they laugh some more, flip through the comic pages and point at something in there I can't see. I watch Burt as he does his cool-dude lean on the magazine rack. I try to use a *Dr. Fantastic* brain surge to make that rack fall right over and take Burt down with it. But no. Burt just keeps looking all cool-like until he and Anna stroll out the front door, without even once glancing back and realizing I'm here.

Word of the day: abhor, verb meaning to regard with horror or loathing; detest. As in, "Farley completely abhors Burt and hopes he falls into the nearest pit of snakes."

24

"FARLEY?" IT'S DAD'S BOOMING VOICE AND HIS big-bam power knock on the door. "Farley? You up yet?"

"Yeah, Dad." I rub my eyes. I'm not even sure how long I've been in here anymore. Could be weeks. Maybe months or years. Maybe I'm actually thirty-five and it's safe to set foot outside again. I glance down at my short, stubby legs tucked under the covers. Okay, maybe not. It's been an entire day. Man, time moves slowly in exile. I'm sure Tomy would agree—who knows how long he'd been trapped in cyberspace before I accidentally released him. But I'm not speaking to him, either. Hope he's enjoying sea monkey life.

"Can I come in?" Dad says.

"Whatever," I say. As if he'll even wait for a response. Dad pushes the door open, squashing *War and*

Peace against the wall. He stands there clad in his running shorts, the ones I didn't rip, a Grady's shopping bag crumpled in his right hand.

"Hey, Dad."

"Hey, Far. I got you something."

He tosses the bag on my bed. It lands in a heap by my feet.

"Aren't you going to see what it is?" he asks.

"Yeah, all right." I pick up the crinkly plastic bag. I'm sure it's too much to hope for the newest *Dr. Fantastic*. Burt and Anna probably got the last one anyway.

I look inside. Blue running shorts, matching shirt, socks, and a fuzzy headband. *Seriously?* I think. *Is this some kind of joke?*

"Seriously?" I say out loud. "Is this some kind of joke?"

"Nope," says Dad. "Get up. Get changed. We're going running. You've made it too far to give up now." *Clap! Clap!*

"Uh-uh. No way. I'm not running. In fact, I'm never leaving my room again. I thought you were aware of that."

"Afraid I'm not taking no for an answer," Dad says. "Get changed and meet me downstairs in five minutes. You're not a quitter. No son of mine is a quitter!"

I stare at Dad in total disbelief, standing there in his sleek running gear. It's like we don't even live on the same planet, let alone in the same house. Suddenly, all those feelings I've spent almost twelve years covering up with jokes and well-timed farts bubble to the surface.

"Yes, I am," I say, softly at first.

"Yes, you are what?"

"Yes, I am." I say, voice getting louder. "A *quitter*."

"Farley . . . ," Dad starts. "No, you aren't."

"Yes. I. Am!" The words are bursting out now, and I can't stop them. "It's *exactly* what I am! Let me see . . . I've quit baseball, karate, football. I even quit badminton, and that's not a real sport!"

"Oh hey, now, listen, Far . . ."

"No! You listen! Haven't you been paying attention my entire life? Don't you *get it*? I don't win at things, Dad. I'm not a winner. I'm. Not. You!"

I yank the covers over my head, hyperventilating. I can't believe I just said all that. Dad probably hates me now. I wait for him to go away. But he doesn't. I can hear him sitting there, slowly breathing.

"Is that how you feel?" he finally says. "Is that how *I* make you feel?"

I shrug under the covers. Dad taps my legs.

"Oh, Far," Dad says. "No. That's exactly the opposite of how I want you to feel. That's exactly the opposite of how I see you." He pauses and sighs. "Sometimes I think

I get so excited to do father-son stuff together that I miss things, and gah . . . I'm not great at this. How about we take that run? Or walk. Whatever you'd like. So we can get some fresh air. And talk?"

I'm about to launch a protest, when I hear something rattle on my desk.

"Mayday, mayday! Can someone help out a dude? I'm locked inside this gnarly—"

I throw off the covers and sit straight up. "Running sounds great!"

Dad jolts back, blinking. The sea monkey tank rattles again. "What was that?" Dad looks around the room. I leap out of bed.

"Nothing. Just one of my computer games. Let me get changed. Privacy, please!" I point at the door and push Dad out.

I put on my running gear and hobble downstairs. Dad's by the front door, jogging in place and boxing the doorknob.

"Far!" he says. "Glad you changed your mind, son. Let's go!"

And he's out the door, with me reluctantly on his tail.

"*Bum-ba-da-dum-da-da-dum-di-dee-dum*," he sings.

Oh man, it's gonna be a long morning. Why did I

agree to this? Oh yeah, that pest in my sea monkey tank.

I trudge behind Dad while he sings and jog-dances. I try to imagine what it's like to be David Turner. To never have to wonder if you're good enough. To always get first place. In everything. Yeah, right. I stand a better chance of actually digging a tunnel to the center of the earth and battling dinosaurs than becoming that guy.

"So, Far," he says, jogging effortlessly. Lawn mowers are busy again with their early-morning rattle. Dad waves at the neighbors, stopping every so often to sign autographs for his swooning fans. "Did I ever tell you how I met your mother?" he asks.

I nod. "Homecoming dance." Geez, I've heard the story only a million times. The perfect David and Meghan, dancing beneath the twinkling disco ball and balloon arch while the rest of the nobodies stared in awe.

"Yeah, but did I tell you how I *really* met her that night?"

I shake my head. I'm getting winded already. The sweet little kids on tricycles are now pointing and laughing. I don't see them exactly. But I'm sure of it. I can hear the cackling over the chirping birds. Word travels fast here on the tree-lined streets of Gentle Cove. It'll travel even faster through the halls at school. I can only imagine what sort of spectacular new names wait for me there. Rip-Fart. Farley Tear-ner. I wonder how Mom feels about homeschooling. Undoubtedly it would make her Very, Very Tired. I'd probably be stupid to even ask.

Ugh, Dad. I want to go home.

"Yeah, a bunch of my buddies and I were break-dancing," Dad says. "Well, actually, my buddy George—"

"Uncle George?" I interrupt. Dad nods. Uncle George isn't exactly my uncle. He's just been Dad's best friend for, like, a million years or so. The guy lives somewhere down South now, but he comes back to Middleford during Thanksgiving break every year. He always stops by to visit Dad, and Mom always immediately sends them out on the patio, even if it's ten degrees out there. Dad and George don't seem to care, though. They'll sit there all afternoon, surrounded by a cloud of cigar smoke, slapping each other's backs, laughing, and probably making cool burping noises. I guess it's not too hard to see why Mom doesn't want them anywhere near her fancy autumn cornucopia display on the kitchen table. I kind of like it though. It's the one time of year Dad acts like a regular person and not all Dad-like.

"Yeah, so Uncle George was break-dancing," Dad says.

I hold back a little laugh. It's sort of hard to picture the bald guy from our back porch with the belly that hangs over his pants doing much more than eating potato chips and drinking soda straight from the can.

"Wow. Uncle George is cool," I say.

"Yeah, super cool," Dad says. "Sometimes a little too cool, you know. There were times I hated even standing next to him."

"Really?"

"Uh-huh. But he was still the best pal a guy could ever have. And when it comes down to it, that's all a person needs in life. One true friend. The rest just falls into place."

I get a little twinge of guilt spying Burt's mailbox off in the distance.

"So what about Mom?" I say, changing the subject. "At the dance. What happened next?"

"Right, yeah, the dance," he says. "So anyway, I see your mom coming up by the refreshment table. Student council had this big thing set up with punch and cookies and stuff." Dad waves his arms around.

"So," he says, "I figure now's my chance. I'm going to get your mother's attention. I'd been practicing my moves all summer. All summer! Even went to break-dancing camp. And bought these really flashy orange metallic MC Hammer pants—don't ask; it's mortifying." He shudders. "So, I had this crazy move planned where

I spin on my head." Dad points at his head, as though I might not know what he's talking about otherwise. "I practiced it a million times on a little piece of cardboard out in Grandma and Grandpa's driveway."

He draws a rectangle shape in the air over the sidewalk. He must think I'm completely daft.

"Anyway," he says. "I shove George out of the way and start flailing in every direction. Then I get to the part where I spin on my head. Only I'm so nervous, I don't really go fast enough to make it all the way around. So I'm stuck in the air with these crazy long, skinny legs flopping everywhere."

He pauses to catch a breath.

"Man," he says with a laugh. "You have no idea how much I hated these legs back then. Bane of my existence."

I look at Dad's perfect form, which is basically a cross between Derek Jeter and Tom Brady, with a little Usain Bolt thrown in for good measure. "Say what?"

"These legs, Far," Dad says. "End of sophomore year. I had a huuuuge growth spurt. Think I grew a half a foot in four months. Which sounds cool, right? Except, it was like all of a sudden I didn't know where my own feet were anymore. Or my head. Or my hands. Missed every pitch, overshot every throw. Tried out for varsity baseball—and got cut. It was . . . the worst. I thought my life was over."

My mouth drops. "You didn't make a team? *You?*"

"'Fraid so, Far."

"But . . . I . . . You never . . . ," I sputter, thinking about all my missed swings at the batting cage. "Why didn't you ever tell me that?"

"I don't know why. I guess I should have," Dad says. "I guess I always thought if you knew I'd failed, you wouldn't be proud of your old man. Kind of stupid of me, wasn't it?"

I'm stunned. I don't even know what to say.

"I fail at plenty of things," he continues. "Didn't pass the bar exam the first time. Or the second. I'm terrible at tests. They make me sweat and forget my own name. I actually broke out in hives before the SATs. But, Far, failing doesn't mean you're a *failure*. It just means you tried. I'm sorry if I ever made you feel otherwise. That's on me, buddy, not you. You are not a failure. Not in any definition of the word."

I still don't know what to say. It's a lot to take in. I can't quite square in my brain the image I've always had of "Perfect Dad" to some nervous guy with skinny legs sweating over a test or worrying that he won't impress Mom.

"C'mon." Dad gives my back a friendly tap. "How about we get moving again? And back to the story."

"Okay."

"So there I am," Dad says. "Spindly legs wobbling around in the air, and what happens next? I tip right over. It was like slow motion. I could feel myself going, but I couldn't do a thing about it. I was like a cartoon character. Landed right on the refreshment table. Hit it just right, too. That punch bowl went flying like it had been launched from a catapult."

"No!"

"Oh yeah," he says. "And it gets worse."

"Worse?"

"Yeah. Guess where that punch bowl landed?"

I think. "On Mom."

"Bingo!" Dad says. He pokes the air with his pointer finger.

"Wow."

"Oh yeah. I figured she must hate my guts. She looked so nice that night. Most beautiful girl I'd ever seen. Like Molly Ringwald," he says, all dreamy-like.

"Who?"

"Oh, never mind," Dad says. "Anyway, your mom's all decked out in this pretty white dress. Pretty white dress that's now all covered in fruit punch."

I laugh a little.

"So then your mom walks over, a sticky orange slice clinging to her hair. And all I can think is 'where do I hide?' Seriously, Far. I would've crawled under the gym bleachers, but they were all pushed back to make room for the dance."

"So what did you do?"

"I stood there like an idiot while George pointed and laughed and made these crazy snorting sounds."

Hmmm, maybe *that's* why Mom actually kicks Dad and George out of the house all the time.

"Yep," Dad says. "But then your mom, she stopped right in front of me, plucked the orange peel off her head, and said, 'If you're going to get me some punch, David Turner, I'd like a cookie to go with it.'" Dad laughs. "And, well, the rest is history."

I don't say anything. I just think as we keep jogging up Gentle Way.

"So, Far, all I'm saying is, you just never know. Okay? People can surprise you."

Yes, they certainly can.

We puff along in silence, and then here we are, right in front of Anna's house.

"You know," he says, slowing down. "Maybe you should go talk to her."

My face turns beet-red. Dad saw Anna in the window yesterday?

"I mean, imagine if I'd succeeded in hiding from

your mom at that dance," he continues. "There might not be a *you*."

"It's not the same," I say. "She probably doesn't even want to talk with me. . . ."

"You don't know that," Dad says. "She's your friend. Come on, Far. You're Rocky Balboa! At the steps of the Philadelphia Museum!" *Pow-pow-ka-pow*. His fists jab an imaginary foe.

"Fine," I say. When Dad starts talking in analogies, all hope is lost. Maybe this is how he actually wins all his cases. Keeps yammering till the judge gives up, the jury goes to sleep, or the defendant just throws himself on the mercy of the court.

I lumber up the brick walkway and tap lightly on the door. No one answers. Oh well. I tried. I spin around to make my getaway. Dad shakes his head and points at the house.

Criminy!

I press the doorbell this time. Footsteps. Voices inside. Oh man.

The door swings open.

Anna stands on the other side. Her red hair is tied up in two little pigtails, just like back in kindergarten, and she looks sweet and sleepy in a pair of pink fuzzy footie pajamas with a little rabbit holding a bunch of flowers on the front.

What time is it anyway? How early did Dad get me up? I smile a shaky half smile and start to raise my hand to wave.

Anna blinks twice and looks down at her fuzzy pink-clad feet. At the very tip of each one is a little white nose with black whiskers sticking out from the sides. Pink bunny ears flop over the top. Anna's eyes grow wide. Her mouth opens. "Oh my . . . Ahhhhh!" She turns and runs up the stairs in a blur.

Great. She can't even stomach looking at me. *Thanks bunches, Dad.* I stand there like a bozo, my feeble wave hanging limply in the air.

Anna's mother appears, holding a spatula in her right hand.

"Hi, Farley," she says. "Sorry. Getting a late start around here this morning. And look at you, out for a run already!" She taps my shoulder and waves the spatula toward Dad on the sidewalk, then looks back up the tall stairs. "Anna! Come back down."

"No!" I hear from somewhere far off in the house. "Why did you have to make me get the door? I hate you!" Something slams.

Super good going, Dad.

"I'm sorry, Farley," Mrs. Murphy says, cheeks flushing. "I'll make sure she calls you later."

"Yeah, uh, okay. Thank you."

I jog right back down the walkway and straight past Dad.

I don't care how many great stories he tells. There's not a single thing he can say now to get me out of my room until I'm eighteen or the EMTs come lift me out with one of those giant cranes.

25

"I AM GETTING KIND OF COOPED UP IN HERE, dude. No room for my daily stretches. I'm very unbalanced!" Tomy turns and attempts a downward dog, bumping his pixelated head on the clear plastic of his sea monkey prison. "See? How about letting a guy out?"

I shake my head, glancing around my own self-imposed prison. "Sorry, buddy," I say. "You got me into this mess. Unless you can figure out a way to get me out of it, we're stuck here together."

"Ah! Is that all?" Tomy says. "The answer is right in front of you!"

I roll my eyes. The only thing I see right in front of me is my bed. "Good idea," I say. "I think I'll take a nap."

"No, dude. I mean the answer!" He points his

miniature finger at my computer. Just like that, the screen lights up and a scroll unfurls with a *whoosh*.

Step Six: Reality Check

"You've got to be kidding me," I say.

Tomy shrugs and points at the computer again. "You have a better idea?"

I sigh. Not really. So I sit down in front of the computer and read. It's not like I have anything left to lose, or anywhere to go.

Your next exercise is to reflect on your goals.
Where are you on your journey? Write down
your progress.

Okay, here goes:

1. Ran all the way to Burt's house. And back in record time. (Even if that doesn't count completely. I was in a hurry. I had no pants.)
2. Climbed a rock wall.
3. Ate a prune.
4. Made a complete and utter fool of myself.

So much for that. Next?

Now take stock of yourself. Write the three
phrases that describe you now. Reflect on
how you've changed since your journey
began.

All right, three things that define me now. That's easy.

1. Still "husky."
2. Dumber than when I started.
3. The furthest thing from brave.

Oh, wait. I'd better add broke to that list. Dad docked my allowance for the next six weeks, thanks to those million-dollar smoothies I had the nerve to put on his tab. Yeah, for all you math geniuses out there, that's thirty bucks. Dad charges interest. Apparently, twenty dollars is *not* an acceptable tip. At least, not if you're the one giving it.

"Well?" Tomy says. "Have you gained any new insights?"

I look at my list. I look at stupid New Farley, still taped to the side of the computer in all his hope and splendor, wearing that ridiculous space suit. I look at Tomy again. He nods sagely, blond hair flowing around his head.

"Yep," I say. "I finally figured out the 'Y' in TomY. . . ."

"Yes!" Tomy says with a fist pump.

"Yes," I say. "There *is* no 'why.'" I pull New Farley off the side of the computer, crumple him up, and toss him in the trash, alongside Old Farley. Maybe they can have a party together down there. Maybe New Farley can eat Old Farley's biscuit hands and feet.

"But . . . !"

"And now I'm going to take that nap."

26

MAN, WHY DOES THE DOORBELL ALWAYS HAVE to ring just when I've finally fallen asleep? Sheesh. I peel the pillow from my cheek and peek out my bedroom window. I bet it's Burt again. Probably coming around to show me the fun pictures he and Anna undoubtedly took together in Grady's photo booth right before they bought the last *Dr. Fantastic.*

But no, I can't tell who it is. All I see is the top of a blond-haired head. And it doesn't belong to Burt.

The doorbell rings again.

Someone better hurry up and get it. I have another 6.05 years until I'm leaving my room again.

Finally, I hear Mom's muted voice and another woman's voice talking. Then Mom says, "Please, come in. It's good to see you."

Footsteps clacking across the foyer. Kitchen chairs scuffling. The refrigerator opening and ice clinking in glasses.

Now Dad's big voice. And he says, "Anna?"

Did Dad say Anna?

"Anna, of course, yes," he booms. "Hi, Jenny. I wanted to say hello earlier today, but Farley ran away too quickly to come up to the door."

My whole body turns to a pile of slush. Well, a bigger pile of slush. I creep toward my door and crack it open a notch.

"Excuse me?" Tomy says from his prison. "About earlier . . ."

"Shhh!" I put my finger to my lips and cup my hand over my ear to get a better listen to what's happening downstairs.

"So," Mrs. Murphy says. "I am terribly sorry to bother you over all this."

"Oh, it's no problem," Mom says.

"I just feel so bad. I don't know what else to do. She won't listen to reason," Mrs. Murphy says.

Mom sighs. "Kids are funny, aren't they?"

Gee, thanks, Mom. You think it's funny Anna's mother can't get Anna to talk to me or to call or whatever it is she wants her to do?

"She just won't come out of her room," Anna's mother says. "Told me she's going to stay in there forever. Wants to sell the house and have Derek rejoin the air force! Request to be stationed in Antarctica."

Wow. That's a harsh response over a pair of *Dr. Fantastic* underpants. I'm definitely never leaving this house.

"She's just so embarrassed," Anna's mother says.

Huh?

"Says I ruined her life with those pink bunny pajamas," she continues. "Don't ask me how. She's the one who picked them out. But what do I know? I'm just her mother, right?"

"Oh, I know," Mom says with another sigh. "It's a tough age. Couldn't pay me to be eleven again."

All the grown-ups laugh.

Double huh?

"So anyway," Mrs. Murphy says. "I was hoping you'd talk to Farley. See if maybe he'd give her a call or something. Stop by. She's so worried about starting school with no friends."

Dad chuckles.

"Well, we just need to get Farley out of *his* room first," he says.

27

THIS TIME IT'S MOM AT MY DOOR. THE LATEST to join the parade of well-meaning Turners. I throw a T-shirt over the tank to hide Tomy. He mumbles something in return.

"SHHHH!" I say as Mom comes into the room.

"Who are you talking to, Far?" she says.

"No one," I say. "What's up?"

"Got a minute?"

"Sure." I sit on the edge of the bed. Mom sits next to me. There's something square clutched in her right hand. She tucks it next to her leg and takes a deep breath.

"So," she says. "Mrs. Murphy came by today."

"Oh yeah?" I try to act like this is news.

"Yeah. She was hoping you'd give Anna a call or maybe stop by."

"I don't know, Mom." I shift so I'm not looking right at Mom's big expectant eyes. "I don't think she really wants to hear from me. Or see me. I think Mrs. Murphy was probably just trying to be nice."

"Oh," she says. "Is that what you think?"

I nod.

Mom's quiet. Apparently she has no argument for this. Might as well be going now. But instead, she shifts around and pulls that square thing out from next to her leg.

"Can I show you something, Far?" Mom's hand lands on my arm.

"Okay, I guess."

She hands me the square. I glance down. It's a picture. A picture of a really goofy girl with the biggest, goofiest smile in probably all of recorded history and the biggest, goofiest buck teeth I've ever laid eyes on. Poor kid. She's wearing a pair of plaid pants, a striped sweater, and a thick purple headband. Only the headband's not actually keeping any hair back; it's just stuck on the top of her head like those silly plastic things from the party store that hold alien antennae. Even worse, she's got a set of ears that stick out at least ten feet on each side.

I can't for the life of me imagine why Mom wants me to see a snapshot of this sorry girl. Unless . . .

"Aww man, Mom. Are you trying to set me up or something?" That's all I need.

"Well, I sure hope not. That would be strange, to say the least. . . ."

Suddenly, the sea monkey tank rattles on my desk. I freeze. Mom spins around just as the tank *thump*s to a stop. She stares for a minute. "Weird," she says. "I could've sworn I saw something moving over there. . . . You didn't secretly get a pet, did you, Farley?"

"No! It's nothing," I say. "Just, uh . . . my laundry pile falling over."

"Farley . . . ," Mom says.

"I know. I know. Hamper in the hallway." I force a nervous smile and change the subject. "So, what's with the picture?"

"Right." Mom shoves it into my hand and grins. "Take a closer look. Notice anything familiar?"

I study the girl. She's holding a book and leaning on a yellow kitchen counter. There's a clunky microwave with giant buttons in the background and an old phone behind her. . . . The kind with the long, twirly cord attached. A big wooden spoon and fork hang on the wall next to a cuckoo clock.

"Hey, wait a minute!" I say. "Is that Grandma and Grandpa's house?"

"Sure is." Mom grins.

"But what's with the old phone? And that huge microwave?"

"It's an old picture," Mom says. "About thirty years old, I'd say."

I look again at the girl's blue eyes. I look at Mom, her blue eyes crinkling around the edges as she grins. I study Mom's perfectly styled hair. Her made-up pink cheeks. Her row of straight white teeth. She smiles wider and nods.

"Nooooo," I say. "Really?"

"Yep, that's me. I'm about ten. Before the braces. And the hairstylist. And before I finally finished growing into those giant ears."

"How come I've never seen a picture like this of you before?"

"Oh, Farley. Let's just say when Meghan McCarthy turned fifteen and got the braces off, she was overcome with a fit of retroactive vanity and got rid of the, uh, evidence. Crazy, I know. At least this one picture survived. When I look at it now, I actually see that this girl was kind of cute. In her own silly way, that is. She's happy, too."

I look over at my Batman trash can and think of poor Old Farley crumpled up and tossed in there like a dirty tissue. And for what reason? For just being Farley. I think this one over and look at Mom again. I inspect the photograph.

"I'm glad that picture survived too. You're right. It is kind of cute."

Mom smiles. "Yep. You know, sometimes we're not really the best judges of ourselves, if you know what I mean. Sometimes we can't see our own selves clearly. Not for a long, long time. It can take a while to grow into the person we're going to become.

"Look, Far," she continues. "I'm not going to tell you that you have to call Anna. I'm not going to tell you to do anything. But I think it would be nice. And I don't think you'll be sorry if you do. Remember, it doesn't feel good to think everyone is laughing at you. So consider it, okay?"

"Okay," I say.

"Good." She stands and pats my knee. "See you when you're ready."

"Okay, Mom."

She walks to the door and nearly trips over that giant *War and Peace* asteroid.

"Mom?"

"Yeah, Far?" she says.

"Do you think you could take that thing back to the library for me?"

She raises an eyebrow. "Done with Tolstoy?"

I nod. "For now. But I was thinking maybe you could get me something else. Something better for an eleven-, well, almost twelve-year-old, you know."

Mom smiles. "I think that's a great idea. I'll go tomorrow. And you can come if you want. If you feel like leaving this room, that is."

"Okay, Mom. Thanks."

She picks up *War and Peace* and starts walking out again. But instead of leaving, she grabs something from the hallway floor and comes back to my bed.

"One other thing," she says. "This was sitting at our front door. I assume it's for you."

She sets the newest *Dr. Fantastic and the Planet of Doom* next to me.

Huh?

"Um, thanks, Mom," I say.

"Sure, honey," she says, heading back out the door. "I'll see you in a bit."

I pick up the *Dr. Fantastic*. A piece of folded paper is clipped to the top. It reads:

> *Farley,*
> *I guess you were right. Maybe I should've let*
> *you have the* Dr. Fantastic *for once.*

Sorry.

Your friend,

Burt

PS. Check out the telepathic mind meld on

page 21. It's awesome!

I flip to the first page. Still crisp and crinkly and glossy. Even so, I don't feel like reading. I get up, pull the T-shirt off my sea monkey tank, and gently lift out Tomy. He resumes the downward dog pose the minute I set him on the desk.

"Ahhhhhh," he breathes out.

"Sorry about that," I say, jiggling my computer mouse. The screen pops to life. There's something I want to see for myself. . . .

I launch YouTube, type "Rocky Theme Song" into the search field, and hit play.

Bum-ba-da-dum-da-da-dum-di-dee-dum!

Would you look at that? There's that Rocky guy. (He doesn't look anything like a rock, by the way—even if he is dressed all in gray. Oh well.) He's running down the street, a bright red headband around his forehead. (Well, I guess now I know where Dad gets his fashion inspiration. . . .)

Tomy stops doing yoga and sits on the edge of my keyboard and watches too.

"This dude shows awesome determination," he says. "Who is he?"

"Rocky," I answer. "He's a fighter."

"Ah, I see," Tomy says. "A *fighter*. Like you."

"Like me?"

The music picks up speed. Rocky's still running and running. Up and down the streets . . . alone. He's doing one-armed push-ups. He's getting punched in the stomach. He's boxing . . . meat? *Eeew!* He's running past trash can fires. But wait! There are a bunch of kids following behind him now. And some more people. And he's still running, faster than anything! And now I think the *entire town* is jogging behind him as he leads them down the city streets, along the railroad tracks, and straight up those steps Dad was babbling about.

The music builds to a crescendo, triumphant.

Bum-bum-buuuum!

Rocky reaches the top and throws his fists in the air.

"Yes!" I leap to my feet and punch mine toward the sky too.

Tomy does the same. His cover-up rises an inch too high. . . .

"Oh!" he says, slapping it down, face red.

Rocky spins in circles, fists still in the air.

And suddenly I begin to get it.

"Yeah. A fighter. Like me."

I sit back down in my chair, retrieve Old Farley from the trash, and smooth him out on my desk. I stare at him for a moment. Funny thing I never noticed before. Old Farley is smiling. A big smile. Even with no ears and biscuit feet, Old Farley looks happy. I grab a pencil from my desk. With renewed determination, I erase Old Farley's baggy shirt and replace it with some sleek running gear. And so what if that super-futuristic stretchy fabric has to stretch a little extra to cover all those layers of Farley? I put a pair of running shoes on the biscuit feet, add some ears, and sketch a rocking guitar around his neck. I hold up the paper and inspect my work.

Looks good, but there's still something missing. Old Farley's surrounded by a lot of blank space. Like that empty street when Rocky started running. I pick my pencil up again. To my right, I draw Burt holding his microphone; to the left, Josh and his drums. I scribble "The Fantastics!" across the top. Now, that's more like it. And what do you know, there's even room there for a keyboard player, I'd say.

I grab some tape and stick my new creation on the side of the computer, right above my "guidepost" list of things to do. I pull that down and inspect it, thinking.

You know, maybe I've been going about this whole thing all wrong. Maybe this wasn't ever about fitting in an astronaut suit, or reading some big book I didn't understand, or trying to be a hero.

Maybe the bravest thing you can do is be yourself.

And just like that, a burst of gold glitter erupts over Tomy's head, and the sixth scroll snaps shut.

"Yes!" We both throw our arms up in the air again, Rocky style, and give each other fist bumps.

"I gotta call Burt now," I say. After all, going solo's not all it's cracked up to be.

"But . . ." I grin at Tomy. "First there's something we need to do. . . . C'mon, grab your surfboard."

Tomy's eyes light up. "Duuuuuuude, no way!"

"Yes way." I point at my hood. "Hop in!"

And before I can even blink, Tomy's breath is tickling the back of my neck as we sneak down the hall. . . .

"Cow-a-bunnnnnnnn-ga!!!"

Tomy executes a perfect Rodeo Flip across the water blasting from the jet in my parents' bathtub, and . . . moons me.

I slap my fingers over my eyes. Not again!

"Oops. Sorry, dude!" a little voice shouts. "Forgot my trunks!"

"It's cool." I laugh. Tomy throws both hands up in the air and makes hang-ten signs.

"Most rad day ever!" he shouts.

"Yeah, it's shaping up to be pretty good," I say, and a little twinge of sadness hits. I don't know how much longer Tomy will be around, but you know what? I'm kind of gonna miss him when he's gone.

28

"I CAN'T BELIEVE YOU GUYS LET A GIRL JOIN the band!" Josh says.

"So?" Burt says. "The band was my idea in the first place."

"Yeah, and if it were up to you, we'd be called the Burt-Tones!" Josh grumbles under his breath. "How are we supposed to be a famous *boy* band if we have a girl in the band?"

"Maybe you should think outside your comfort zone," I say.

"What does that even mean?" Josh says.

"It means she's cool," Burt answers.

"Whatever." Josh picks at a square sticker remnant and wobbles on his puny drum stool. "I still say it's bad for our image."

Mr. Chan hollers from the kitchen, "Boys, your friend is here!"

In a matter of moments, Anna breezes into the garage, holding a portable keyboard under her right arm. A real keyboard. Not the toy kind.

Suddenly, the toy guitar hanging from my neck feels completely ridiculous.

"It's just for practice," I say with a shrug, glancing down at the tiny instrument.

"Oh." Anna inspects the guitar and a half smile creeps across her face. She taps her tie-dyed high-top on the garage floor. "I like it. It's kinda fierce. In an ironic sort of way, you know."

I'm pretty sure I turn the color of a cherry tomato.

"Hey!" Josh shouts. "My drums are also a practice set! See?" He taps what's left of the red sticker and does this weird grin-snort combo.

Burt rolls his eyes at me.

Anna sets up her keyboard on a folding table and pulls a microphone from her side pocket.

"Here," she says, handing it to Burt. "The sound comes through the keyboard speakers."

"Awesome!" Burt taps the microphone. "Check. One, two. Check." He blows into the top, and metallic puffs of Burt breath emerge from the keyboard. "Cool!" he says.

Josh taps the cymbal triangle. "A one, a two, a one, two, three."

Bum-bum! Bum-bum-de-da-dum! My guitar wails. I do my signature move and accidentally knock a ball from the shelving unit. It rolls underneath the car. Josh's cat materializes out of nowhere and chases after it.

"Wild thing!" Burt sings, jumping off a low chair. "You make my fart sing!"

"Heart!" Josh yells. "You make my 'heart' sing, you idiot!"

Anna tosses her hair and her sweet snort-laugh fills the garage. She runs her fingers over the keyboard. Sprinkles scampers from under the car with a screech and dashes outside.

After practice we sit by Josh's pool. Anna smoked us all in the burping contest once again. And this time I actually tried. At least Burt didn't wet his pants. He knew what to expect.

"So, are we gonna swim or what?" Anna asks. She motions toward the pool. "Bet I can do a better cannon-ball than you, Far."

"Game on!" I say.

"Farley!" Mr. Chan yells from the kitchen window. "Your mom is here."

Darn. Great timing, Mom.

"Okay," I say. I push back my plastic chair. It scrapes across the cement patio in protest. "Guess I've gotta go. I'll see you guys at my party."

"See ya Saturday, Fart," Josh says.

"Bye, Far," Burt says.

Anna waves.

I walk through the sliding door into Josh's basement. I'm almost to the bottom of the stairs when a hand with glitter-polished nails catches my shoulder. I spin around.

"Hey, Farley." It's Anna.

"Oh. Hi," I say.

Anna looks at the ceiling for what seems like a million years. I look too, to see what's so interesting up there. Just a lightbulb. Okay . . . I look back at Anna. She's still watching the light.

"I just wanted to thank you," she finally says.

"For what?"

"Uh, for inviting me to join the band. For being my friend." She looks at her feet. Her big toe draws a small circle in the carpet. "And, uh, for not telling anyone about, uh, you know, the footie pajamas." Her eyes meet mine.

"Yeah, sure, it's okay." I shrug. "I don't know what the big deal is, though. You looked cute."

Anna's hand lands on my arm.

"Thanks. You're cute too." Her hand doesn't move.

I blink about one hundred million times and something that sounds like, "duh, uh, uh, guh," comes out of my mouth. Cute? Nobody's ever called me cute before. Except Mom. And Great-Aunt Alice. And that's only because they're required to. It's the law or something. Anna smiles.

"Farley!" It's my mother's voice from the top of the stairs. "Let's go! Your father's waiting in the car! He's got the engine running."

"Yeah, yeah, okay!" Better not make David Turner waste gas. That costs money.

Anna's hand slips back next to her waist and fiddles with the bow on her bathing suit.

"Bye, Farley," she says. "See you this weekend." Her mouth twists to the side and back. She looks up at the light again. Then suddenly she leans over and kisses my cheek. And without another peep, she runs right back through the open sliding glass door and does a massive cannonball into the pool. My hand flies to my face.

"Garg, fargle, urgle, garg."

"FARLEY ANDREW TURNER!" Mom hollers.

Oh boy. Time to move it. Mom's invoked my middle name.

I hightail it up the stairs to the best of my wobbly

kneed ability, run past Mom, and lurch into the back seat of the car.

"Hey, Far!" Dad says. "How was practice?"

"*Garg, fargle, urgle, garg*," I say, eyes still wide, hand still clutched to my hot cheek.

"Good to know, son," Dad says. "Good to know."

Mom slides into the passenger seat and looks at Dad's grinning face. "What's going on in here?" she asks. She turns around and looks at me, then back at Dad.

"Father-son talk," he says. He catches my eye in the rearview mirror and gives me a knowing nod, and I slowly return his smile.

"Yeah, father-son talk."

29

MY BIRTHDAY PARTY IS NOT TILL TOMORROW, but my actual birthday is today. So me, Mom, and Dad are opening family presents in the living room. We're seated on our big brown leather sofa, me in the middle, Mom to my left, Dad to my right. A pile of presents is stacked on the coffee table in front of me. I already opened Grandma and Grandpa Turner's. They sent a Tickle Me Elmo and dinosaur socks.

I'm pretty sure they think I turn four every year.

Dad hands me the next gift, a small red-wrapped box. I check out the square card with a big blue balloon on top. It's from him. I tear the package open, sending red paper flecks flying, and blink about a million times when I reach the white box inside.

"Awesome! My own iPod! Thanks, Dad!" I fumble

it from the packaging and push the power button. The screen illuminates with an explosion of pixelated stars. "Whoa. And you got me the special Dr. Fantastic edition?!"

Dad smiles and nods.

Mom peers over my shoulder. "Oooh, that looks cool," she says. "Does it have Tetris on it?"

I snap the iPod close to my chest. "Forget it, Mom!"

"Ah, all right," she says.

"There *are* a bunch of exclusive Dr. Fantastic apps and games preloaded on there, though," Dad says. He puts his arm around my shoulder. "Maybe you could show me how to play a couple? I really enjoy hanging out together. And our talks."

"Me too," I say. "That would be awesome."

"Yeah, awesome," Dad says, and I think maybe he's blinking back tears. "I'm proud of you, Far. I've *always* been proud of you."

"Thanks, Dad," I say. "This is the best birthday present ever!"

And the funny thing is, I don't mean the iPod.

Dad pulls me in for a hug. "You're welcome, buddy. Thank *you*. You make me a better person, you know. I'm so lucky to have you as a son."

I lean into him. I can't remember the last time Dad

and I really hugged—not since I was a little kid with a skinned knee, I guess. Sometimes I think there are lots of things fathers and sons don't do—or say to each other—maybe because we think we're not supposed to. I don't know. But I'm not going to be afraid to tell Dad what's on my mind anymore. I hug him back. Tight. And it's the best feeling ever.

Dad lets me go with a tap on the shoulder, and Mom starts bouncing around like it's her birthday too. Either that or the couch just caught on fire. She grabs a giant package off the table and plops it on my lap.

"This one's from me!" She rubs her hands together. "Open it, honey!"

I rip off the confetti wrapping paper, hands sweating in anticipation. Underneath I find a wide cardboard box that's been taped tightly shut. I pull at the tape to no avail. There must be eight thousand yards of it covering every possible inch of the package. Mom really loves tape. I tug at a big wad with a long blond hair wound up in it. Ew.

"Sorry." She smiles sheepishly.

"It's okay, Mom."

I keep pulling till finally I'm able to rip a corner of the box open. I reach my hand in and feel something soft, like, like . . . ugh, clothes.

Like usual.

Darn. Oh well. As excited as she looked, I thought maybe Mom had gotten me something different this year. But no, Mom always gets me new clothes for back to school. Major disadvantage of having a birthday right before Labor Day. At least it's not as bad as Josh, though. His birthday's right before Christmas. Talk about a rip-off.

I practice my happy face in my mind so I don't look too disappointed.

Keeping one eye on my awesome new iPod for inspiration, I extract a black T-shirt from the box. At least it's not yellow with polka dots. I drop that on the table and immediately go for the next bunched-up garment thing.

"Thanks, Mom." I force a big smile.

"No, wait, Far! Open it up. Have a look at it!" she says. She waves her hand at the balled-up black lump and starts bouncing around again.

"Okay." I unfold the shirt and hold it in front of my face.

Wow.

Double wow!

Across the top in neon letters I read THE FANTASTICS! And underneath, there's an awesome gold and red logo that looks like a lightning bolt shooting from a rocking guitar neck.

"Mom! This is so cool!" I say.

Mom smiles and rubs her hands together. "Go on!" she says. She points at the box. "There's one in there for you, Burt, Josh, and Anna!"

I pull the other three out. "These are awesome!"

"Thanks, honey."

"Where did you get these?"

"I made them for you, sweetie," she says. "I *am* a graphic designer, you know. People actually pay me to do stuff like this. And the sewing club doesn't only sit around drinking wine." She sticks her tongue out at Dad.

"Hey!" he says. "I never said that!"

Mom grins.

"These are the best! Thanks, Mom," I say again.

"You're welcome. That's not everything, though. . . ."

She reaches behind the couch and starts to pull something huge up and over the back. "Didn't have quite enough wrapping paper," she says with a grunt. "Or tape . . ."

She lets out a loud breath and sets the thing in my lap with a giant smile. My eyes widen. I can't believe what I'm seeing.

"Is this what . . . ?" I start.

Mom nods.

I run my hands over the hard black surface of the

case. It's covered in all these really cool stickers that look like they're from old bands: the Psychedelic Furs, Minor Threat, the Cure. I picture a new one right smack in the middle that reads, THE FANTASTICS!

"Where did you get this?" I ask Mom.

"It's mine," she says, smile pressing so far into her cheeks I think she might permanently relocate her ears to the back of her head. She taps a Modern English sticker. "Ah, I used to love these guys when I was your age. . . . *I'll stop the world and melt with you . . . .*" She sings to herself, then sighs and pulls her hand away. "Go on. Open the case."

I flip the metal latches in disbelief. Inside, cradled in the velvety lining, is a red and white Fender electric guitar. My jaw drops. "I can't believe this is yours. . . ."

"Well, it's yours now," Mom says, still grinning. "Unless Girl Power . . . that's spelled G-R-L P-W-R—we were too post-punk for vowels—decides to do a reunion tour. But, you know, Trish was just promoted to CFO, and Kathy is pretty busy with the triplets." She winks.

I don't think I'm going to be able to pull my jaw off the floor. "You were in a *band*?!"

"Mmm-hmmm," Dad says. "Was she ever . . . Your mom really knows how to rock. And that blue streak in her hair matched her eyes perfectly. . . ." That crazy

Molly-what's-her-name look from our jog washes over his face again.

"C'mon, Far," Mom says, standing. "Let's get this thing set up. I'll teach you a few easy chords. Only need three to make a song. And I hear there might be a concert tomorrow. . . ."

I'm utterly speechless.

Wait till Burt hears.

Word of the day: ecstatic. Ecstatic, adjective, meaning feeling great rapture or delight. *Ecstatic.*

You don't really need a sentence for that one, now, do you?

Yeah, I didn't think so.

30

Step Seven: Keep Moving Forward!
So, you've made it to the end of this journey.
Perhaps you've reached all of your goals.
Perhaps you have modified your plans.
Perhaps you have new goals. The important
thing to remember is the end of one journey
is merely the beginning of another. Look
ahead! Where do you want to go next? The
only limit on you is the one you place on
yourself!

We've got almost all of Mrs. Chittenden's rising seventh-grade class here in my backyard, surrounded by two million balloons, a big cake, and a table full of presents. Dad's at the edge of the patio, burning burgers and hot dogs on his fancy grill. He can cook about fifty things at once on that huge thing. It's even got a special stick to twirl a whole chicken on, not that Dad's ever used that part. In fact, Dad barely ever uses his grill. Mom bought it for him a couple years ago for his birthday, probably hoping for a break from boiling all the time.

But so far Dad's only taken it out for my birthday party and once on Memorial Day. Afterward he spent about twenty hours scrubbing all the black burners and shiny knobs with a special wire brush so it looked brand-spanking-new again.

"Got some fresh wieners here!" Dad yells. He adjusts his KING OF THE GRILL apron and holds a big white tray of shriveled hot dogs in the air.

A huge line forms at the chip bowl.

Dad turns his attention to a lopsided stack of hamburger patties, which he tosses with flair onto the grill. The meat sizzles and a blast of smoke puffs into the sky. A loud bell probably goes off at the fire department. Cows the next town over faint in their fields.

"Cool party," Burt says. He's rolling his microphone between both hands. "When do we jam?"

"After the cake," I say.

"Oh man!" Burt stuffs the microphone into his pocket. He glances around the backyard. He nods toward

Addison, who's standing in a little huddle with the girls on the patio.

"I think I'm gonna go say hello," he says. "See what she thinks of lead singers."

"Cool," I say, and slug him on the back.

As Burt wanders off, presumably to let Addison know the answer to her survey question is "girl C," Anna slides up next to me.

"Hi, Farley," she says.

"Garg, fargle, urgle, garg." Uh, I mean, "Hello."

Anna smiles and reaches into her front pocket. "I know your present table is over there." She points over my shoulder. "But I have something special for you. And I didn't want it to get lost."

She hands me a small wrapped box.

"Thanks," I say.

"Open it!"

"Okay."

I slide the paper away and inspect the small, clear box left in my hands. There's a tiny fleck of something gray inside. What is it? A secret spy microprocessor chip? A magic pill?

"It's a space rock," Anna says.

"What?" I look up.

"A space rock." She smiles. "Well, a piece of a meteorite. A tiny one. But it's the real thing. I figured maybe you'd like this. Until you can go collect them yourself, you know."

"Wow! This is awesome!" I flip the box over in my hands and stare at the rock from all sides. It's got shiny little specks of silver and blue in it. I wonder if it's radioactive. Maybe it will give me special powers or turn me into Superman. That would be cool. "How did you get this?"

"Friend of my dad's." Anna shrugs. "From back at the Air Force Academy, you know. He works for NASA now."

"Wow," I say again. *"Garg, fargle, urgle, garg."*

Fortunately, before I can make any more brilliant remarks, Mom rolls by with a square table on wheels. It's holding a bunch of paper plates and a chocolate frosted cake shaped like a giant guitar. On top, Mom wrote "Happy Birthday, Farley" in gold and red letters.

"Cool cake, Farley!" Anna says.

My mom claps. "Okay, everyone! Time to sing!"

Everyone circles around me and the cake and belts out "Happy Birthday." Mom gives me the first piece—my favorite—the end one with all the extra squiggles of frosting around it.

"Happy birthday, honey," she says.

I nervously inspect the plate in my hand. It's the first cake I've held in almost six weeks. What if I finish this piece and can't stop? What if I feel compelled to knock down the rest of the kids at the party, wheel the entire cake into the garage, and scarf it down in one sitting? What if I can't help myself? What if . . . ?

Nah. It's just a piece of cake. It's not the boss of me.

I am.

And you know what? I deserve to have delicious things too.

I shimmy my fork through the chocolaty layers, tear off a big bite, close my eyes, and sigh as it melts in my mouth.

It's the best darn cake I've ever tasted.

When I'm done, I run to my room to change into my band gear.

"Tomy," I say, putting my meteorite on the desk. "You aren't going to believe this!"

Silence.

"Tomy?" I say. No answer.

The sea monkey tank is empty. Only the mouse sits on my mousepad. The underpants hammock sways in the breeze. No sign of Tomy. Anywhere. My heart sinks. I didn't even get a chance to say Aloha. . . .

For a minute I wonder if I just imagined my miniature friend. Maybe that's what "manifest" actually means. I'll have to check Dad's dictionary. . . .

But then the computer screen flashes. A large scroll unfurls:

> *Right on, dude! Journey complete. Until*
> *the next wave, remember: The path to*
> *enlightenment always begins with YOU!*
> *That is the "Y."*

Tomy's bodyless head reappears in the corner. He nods and smiles. The screen goes black, there's a puff of gold glitter around the monitor, and Tomy disappears completely.

I nod and smile too.

Then I reach around and plug my computer back into the wall.

"And now for something extra special," Dad booms from the patio steps. "Intro-doooo-cing . . . the Fantastics!"

Burt, Josh, Anna, and I come out from behind the half-built fort wearing our awesome new matching outfits. All our band stuff is set up in a special spot Mom cleared out for us over by the relaxation garden.

I pick up my new guitar and crank it full blast. Burt

flips on the microphone with a loud *screech*. Anna's fingers hover over the keyboard. Josh taps his cymbal.

"A one, a two, a one, two, three!"

Bum-bum, bum-bum-de-bum-bum!

"Wild thing!" Burt hollers into his shiny mic. "You make my fart sing! You make everything a moooo-vie!"

I swear I can see Josh's eyes rolling into his head behind me.

"Yeah, yeah, yeah, Wild Thing!" Burt continues.

I lift my right arm high into the air and bring it down with a super swing over the guitar, then sweep my fingers over my eyes. My signature move. The crowd goes wild. Anna swoons. Her legs wobble and she steadies herself with the keyboard. Kaitlyn Duggan passes out. Addison grabs a handful of napkins, holds them to her face, and weeps with joy.

Okay, maybe not quite.

Maybe Grandpa Andrew's actually got those ear speakers turned all the way down since he's just standing there, smiling and nodding, clapping completely offbeat. And maybe the girls are still just huddled over by the punch bowl, probably discussing how cute Burt looks in his wicked cool Fantastics T-shirt. And maybe Mom and Dad are just dancing all goofy-like up front 'cause I'm their kid and they love me.

But it's all good.

We rock.

Hard.

And Anna kissed my cheek. My cheek. Farley Andrew Turner's round, happy cheek. So take that, haters! My arm flies up again and I kick my foot in the air. I spin around and shake my Planet of Doom at the crowd. I play the same three chords Mom taught me last night, over and over, not necessarily in the correct order.

But it's still all good.

Because *I* rock.

Wild thing! Yeah, yeah, yeah, yeah!

ACKNOWLEDGMENTS

Farley began as a character who sprang from my imagination (and heart) eight years ago when I was just beginning my journey as an author. I could very much relate to Farley's desire to be different, special . . . *better*. (Rejections will do that to a person, after all!) But as Farley taught me, persistence pays off. Seven years after Farley first popped into my head, inspiration hit again (like a bad burrito, as Farley would say): Farley's sidekick, Tomy, was born, and *Project Me 2.0* became a real book.

For that, I have many wonderful people to thank:

My fabulous agent, Sarah Davies, who plucked an early version of Farley from the slush pile and took a chance on me, an unknown author. Huge thanks to my brilliant and funny editor, Amy Cloud (or as I like to say, my own personal Tomy!), for helping me dig deep beneath the layers of *PM 2.0* and bring the heart of Farley's quest to the surface. My sincere gratitude to editorial director Fiona Simpson, who brought this project across the finish line without missing a beat; Octavi Navarro, who created the

ACKNOWLEDGMENTS

amazing pixel art cover; and, of course, the many behind-the-scenes folks at Aladdin who ensured this book was free of wEird Random capitAlization, and str,ay commas, and was perfectly typeset, marketed, and sent into the world!

Heartfelt thanks to authors T. P. Jagger and Marci Lyn Curtis for your fantastic beta reads, critiques, and most of all, encouragement to keep going! And hugs to Lisa Maxwell for the excellent writerly chats over green curry and Thai iced tea.

Finally, my never-ending gratitude to the people I hold closest to my heart: my husband, Ted; my mom, Winnie; my dad, Barry; my brother, Greg; my extended family; and especially my kids, Sven and Ava. May you—and every kid who picks up Farley's story—always know that you are loved, worthy, and perfect just as you are, because the bravest thing you can do on this wild and wonderful journey through life is be *yourself*.

Three unlikely friends find themselves
braving the wilderness in search of the mythical
Beast of Bear Falls. Can they uncover the truth
about the Sasquatch living there?

AH, THE FIRST GLORIOUS DAY OF SUMMER BREAK!

I'd managed to survive yet another year of brain-numbing homework, fill-in-the-circle-completely test forms, and whatever that stuff is that the cafeteria workers stick in Sloppy Joes.

Curled snugly in my nice warm bed, I was groggily considering all the things I'd do today: sleep till noon, shower in the lawn sprinkler, spend all afternoon lounging in the California sunshine . . .

HONK!

I bolted upright, whacking my head on the bunk above me. My eyes watered, my legs twitched, and my heart tried desperately to eject itself from my rib cage.

Honk! Honk-it-y-honk-honk-honk!

This was definitely *not* on the list.

I fumbled in the darkness for the clock. . . . No, that *had* to be wrong. 6:47 a.m.

Huh? I held the glowing numbers closer to my face and blinked.

Six. Forty. Seven. *a.m.?*

HONKKKKK!

I dropped the clock. Was this some kind of joke?

"Luiz, my man!" I heard Dad from somewhere downstairs, followed by the front door slapping open and shut.

Who in the heck was Luiz? And why was my dad speaking in that ridiculous voice?

And then it all came flooding back. The truth I'd been trying to block out. The weekend *trip*.

Not Luiz . . . not already. He wasn't supposed to arrive until morning, and in my book 6:47 a.m. was *not* morning. It was definitely the tail end of the middle of the night.

I yanked the covers over my head. Next thing I heard was the sound of Dad's feet thundering up the stairs. *Urgh.* Did he always have to be so . . . enthusiastic? I peeked from beneath my blankets, eyes darting around the room in desperation.

One dresser. One second-story window. One bookshelf. And one truly pathetic-looking half-deflated beanbag chair.

Nowhere to run. Or hide. I flattened myself to the bed. Maybe if I kept real still, Dad wouldn't notice. . . .

I heard the door fly open. Whatever happened to privacy? Clearly I needed to invest in better security. A mantrap perhaps. Even a lock would do.

"Come on, sleepyhead!" Dad said with a clap.

I continued to play dead.

"I wonder where the little guy's got to," Dad said in the kind of silly voice usually reserved for six-year-olds. "I guess Paul musta packed his bags and left home for the summer. Oh well, I guess I'll have to go have fun without him."

Then, my covers were whipped off, leaving me clutching only my pillow. I opened one eye.

Dad stood there wearing a big goofy grin and an outfit ripped straight from the pages of a Wildlife Enthusiast catalog: khaki shorts, khaki vest covered with fishing lures, and coordinating khaki hat plastered with hooks, feathers, and fishing bobs.

He dropped the blankets, went to the window, then whipped open the curtains. I screamed like a vampire exposed to light for the first time. Dad just laughed. The shiny metal pieces on his vest reflected the early morning sunlight in every direction, making him look like some sort of camouflage disco ball.

"Time to get up, Paulie! You haven't forgotten about Bear Falls, have you?"

"I tried," I mumbled. "Really, really hard."

"At least you're dressed," said Dad. "That's the spirit, buddy boy! As the Boy Scouts say, Always Be Prepared!"

That had nothing to do with the trip. I just couldn't be bothered to get undressed the night before, so I was still wearing my favorite long-sleeved Green Day T-shirt and nicely wrinkled cargo shorts. Wearing my clothes in bed also prevents Mom from getting near them. Because Mom irons *everything*: jeans, T-shirts, underwear, potted plants. Nothing's safe in the Adams house. Basically, the only way to avoid looking like Mark Twain Middle School's reigning King of Starch is to break my clothes in overnight. I mean, it's bad enough being twelve sometimes. The last thing I need is to be known as the twelve-year-old with the crease in his socks.

The clock hit 6:48. Dad just stood there, not taking the hint.

I sighed and sat up. I tried to smile, but it probably looked more like a grimace.

Dad winked. "Let's find your backpack, buddy." He went to my closet.

"Hey, don't go in—"

But he'd already opened the door. Hey, he couldn't

say he wasn't warned. All my stuff—clothes (some clean, some not so much), sports gear, stacks of comics, old computer games, semiretired sneakers—came pouring out in an avalanche, burying him and swamping his cries. He came up like a drowning man, with an old jockstrap on his head. And somehow he was still grinning. He shook the stuff off and held out my backpack.

"Let's get cracking! Want to hit the road before traffic picks up!"

"Really? Do I have to, Dad?" I said. "I mean, I'm not much of a camper." I rubbed my crusty eyes again and coughed. "Or a morning person. How about I just stay here? I'll probably just drag you, uh, *outdoorsmen* down anyway."

Dad grinned and shook his head.

"I'll do extra chores for a month."

Another shake. The fishing lures clanked together.

"A year?"

Dad put his hands on his hips.

"The rest of my life!"

"Oh, come on, Paul. It'll be fun!" Dad said. "You wait and see!"

And this time, his smile faltered just a little, and he looked kind of desperate, so I stopped fighting. I knew Dad would never say it outright, but this trip meant a lot to him. He'd been working his butt off for the last year at school, taking on extra classes in the hope of a promotion to head of his department. Just a couple of days ago, they'd told him the job was going to someone else. All those late nights and weekends marking papers and preparing lessons had been for nothing. He pretended it didn't matter, but I knew my parents were worried about money—Mom had been laid off three months ago.

But "fun"? Let's just say Dad and I don't quite share the same definition of "fun." Like last summer, I wanted to go to the Super Mega Blast Water Park and ride the Cannon Shooter. Instead, Dad hauled me off to this tumbledown cabin in the middle of nowhere that was the childhood home of some Really Important Historical Figure who died three hundred years ago. Probably of boredom.

Don't get me wrong; it's not like I don't respect the past and all. But with a history teacher for a dad, it kinda goes without saying I've seen enough Musty Old Places of Historical Significance to last an entire lifetime.

"Okay, chop-chop!" Dad said. He tossed the bag toward me and headed back into the hall, whistling "Yankee Doodle."

I plucked clothes from my dresser and floor and

jammed them into my backpack, doing my best to squash any creases out of them. I was almost done when there was a knock on the door. "Hello, honey," Mom's voice said sweetly. "I have something special for you since you had to be up so early!"

Yes! Maybe this morning wasn't a total bust after all. I wondered if she'd made me pancakes. Or waffles. Or those little French toast things cut into triangles. I flung open the door expectantly and discovered . . .

Mom, standing there in her yellow bathrobe, holding a black T-shirt by the shoulders. "Father and Son Xtreme Adventures" was written across the front.

"Here!" she said. "I ironed this for you!" She pressed the still-warm garment to my chest. I crept back a step.

"Um, yeah, I don't think so," I said.

"Oh, come on," Mom said, raising it to put it over my head. "You'll look cute!"

Cute? Just what any self-respecting twelve-year-old wants to hear. "No, thanks," I said.

"I insist." Mom smiled. She held the T-shirt like it was a net and I was a wild creature about to be captured.

"But—"

"It'll make your dad happy."

I listened to the sound of my dad's whistling in the hallway.

"He sounds pretty happy already," I said.

"*Paul,*" said Mom sternly. "This means a lot to him."

Ugh. Guilt trip coming. "I know," I said. "The job—"

"Not just that," said Mom, lowering her voice. "He feels bad because you guys never spend any time together."

"We watched a Giants game just last week!" I protested.

"*Quality* time," said Mom. "Sitting side by side shouting at the TV doesn't count."

She was right, I guess. There was a point when Dad and I did tons together—swimming, baseball, or just hanging out at the mall. When I was a couple of years younger, we even used to jam together in the garage while he taught me guitar. I'd lost interest, though. Between school, friends, and video games, I didn't have much time for Dad these days.

"Come on, Paul, do it for me," said Mom.

"Yeah, okay," I muttered, lifting my arms.

"Great! He'll be so happy!"

The world disappeared for a second as she put the T-shirt over my head.

Sadly, when it reappeared, nothing had changed.

ABOUT THE AUTHOR

Jan Gangsei grew up in the hills of Vermont, where she began her career as a journalist and photographer. After stints in Key West, New York City, Barbados, and suburban DC, Jan finally settled with her family back in Vermont near the shores of Lake Champlain, where she writes full time. Her debut novel, *Zero Day*, is a political thriller set in her former backyard of Washington, DC. She is also the author of *The Wild Bunch*.